SPEAR

In the same universe:

Slay: An Erotic Tale
Silk: An Erotic Tale

For some queer time-travel adventure…
Check out the Turning Points series
at jodielane.com

The Siege of Masada
Transylvanian Knight
To Kill An Emperor
Renaissance Woman
Heart and Stomach of a Queen

and

The Dark Office
(with Turning Points short stories)

SPEAR

AN EROTIC TALE BY

MICHELLE MARIPOSA

Spear © 2026 Jodie Lane
Cover Design © 2026 1231 Publishing

All rights reserved. No part of this publication may be
reproduced, stored in a retrieval system, or transmitted in
any form or by any means electronic, mechanical,
photocopying, recording, or otherwise, without prior written
permission of the author.

The characters and events portrayed in this book are
fictitious or are used fictitiously. Any similarity to real
persons, living or dead, is purely coincidental and
unintentional.

ISBN: 978-1-7641379-2-8

Published by Jodie Lane
www.jodielane.com

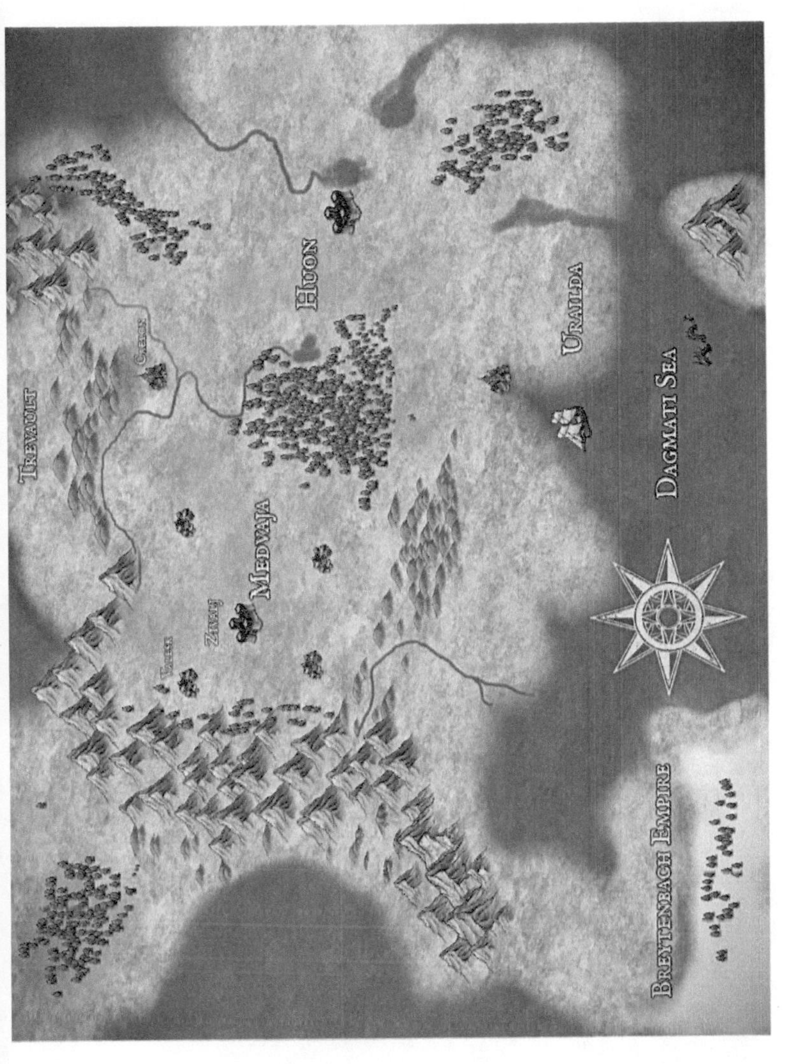

Medvaja and surrounding lands

When the heart is strong, the sword arm cannot falter.

One

Phoenix glances at me in surprise as he returns from the wash room down the inn hall. "You still here?" He runs a hand through his dark curls, still mussed with drying sweat.

My smile fades, and suddenly the bed that smells of us is uncomfortable. "I, uh…" I clear my throat. "Just waiting for the washroom." I had cleaned myself up with a rag, hoping for lazy embraces and conversation into the night.

"Of course." His handsome face belies his polite words—it seems my welcome has expired, and I hurriedly dress, feeling like a hound caught misbehaving.

"Uh, Phoenix?"

"Yeah?" He sounds bored.

"I'll be at the camp with the other Huonese… If you want to see me again." *Do I sound pathetic?*

"Sure thing, Ivan." He plonks himself down on the bed, twitching a blanket over his muscled form.

It's Eitel, not Ivan. Slipping into my jacket and boots, cradling my weapons belt, I let myself out.

I avoid the gazes of soldiers and civilians alike in the inn's common room, envying them staying in the warm and dry. I'm reluctant to return to the wet fields outside the town where my company is camped, but my sergeant will ream me if I stay out much later. Slinging my cloak about me, I trudge out of the inn towards the town square. *It's fine. You had some fun, he doesn't have to want anything more.* It takes a moment to hear the commotion that rips my attention from my own self-pity.

"Get down!"

"To arms!"

Drawing my army-issued short sword, I bolt for the source of the panic. The square is lit with torches, which sizzle in the misting rain, but I can't see the attack past the crowd.

A strident voice hollers, "Stand down!"

"What's going on?" I demand of the Medvajan soldier next to me.

He's too short to see and snaps back, "Cursed if I know!" so I shove my way through until astonishment halts me. Fear grips my heart as I behold the middle of the square.

"Lower your weapons!" The owner of the strident voice sits on the neck of a dragon. She's a hard-faced Medvajan soldier, but I barely notice more than that—it is the huge beast that commands my attention. A creature with scales that shimmer the darkest green in the flickering torchlight. It takes up half the square, even with wings folded tightly to its side. While it has not bared its teeth, claws the length of daggers grace powerful forepaws and all I can think about is how quickly those huge jaws could dart out and rip me in two.

"Kyan? Anasta?" Princess Rhea, commander of the Medvajan forces and heir to her father's throne, strides forth, the crowd parting for her. My own Prince Gereon is right behind her. Her confidence in approaching the great beast calms the surrounding soldiers, who finally lower their weapons.

"Your Highness!" The soldier on the dragon slides to the ground and bows. "Captain al Stauberg sent me to escort Kyan to see you." She's soaked to the skin, and shivering. I move forward without thinking, shrugging free from my cloak and laying it on her shoulders. I'm a big man, and it dwarfs her, but she nods her appreciation of its warmth.

"Princess Rhea, Prince Gereon," the dragon speaks—a deep, mellow voice that has me leaning forward instinctively, drawn to its richness. His warm scent infiltrates the chill air, and I cover my astonishment with a cough.

"Kyan." The Medvajan princess reaches out a hand in greeting. The dragon touches it with his forepaw, then repeats the gesture with Prince Gereon.

Princess Rhea asks, "What brings you here?"

"I understand your countries are at war," the dragon announces, addressing not just the royals, but the whole square. "While my council is reluctant to risk draconic lives, I have dispatched your brave captain and court artist to our Weyr in the hope of convincing my people that our new allies are worth assisting." He swings his head around slowly, looking frightened humans in the face. "I have not yet had the privilege of meeting most of you, but it would sadden me greatly to lose the opportunity before I get the chance. I know many of my dragon kin feel the same."

It takes a few moments for his words to sink in. Everyone is still getting over their astonishment that the dragon can speak, let alone so eloquently.

"What do you propose?" Gereon asks. He's a handsome man, one I'd happily approach if he weren't a prince and I a common soldier. I suffice with fantasies instead.

"I would like to send some of my kin to assist with the bringing of supplies," Kyan the dragon declares. "Flooded rivers and sodden roads are no barrier to our wings."

Excited murmurings spring up behind me. No one wants to be trapped in Caelon under siege, shivering and starving.

Princess Rhea raises a hand, and silence falls. "How could we repay such kindness?"

The silence behind me becomes very still.

Kyan nods. "Your artist, Monique Yulic, has shown those of my wing a glimpse into human culture. I would like to bring more craftspeople back to the Weyr, so others may understand the skills humans possess at building and making tools and other devices."

Princess Rhea flicks her eyes to Gereon, who gives a barely perceptible nod. "You guarantee their safety, of course," she murmurs.

Kyan bows his head. "As you do for my kin."

"It would have to be volunteers," she raises her voice. "Brave souls who venture into the unknown to demonstrate their talents and craftsmanship."

"From Huon, as well," Gereon adds. "There would be much benefit in opening trade to both our lands."

"I shall go," says the soldier who flew in on the dragon. "I come from a family of bowyers, and know the trade."

I glance behind me, to see if anyone else is mad enough to step forward. A tall figure catches my eye—Phoenix, hair mussed, shirt half-tucked. His casual handsomeness is accentuated by his disheveled state.

"I will go." My voice sounds before the thought even occurs to me. "I help the blacksmiths in the armory." They don't need to know that's because blacksmiths have *amazing* muscles—I know the army is full of sweaty men but something about the quiet concentration of blacksmiths has me longing.

Prince Gereon casts an eye over me, noting my size, my uniform, and gives a nod.

"I shall have more volunteers by morning," the princess informs Kyan. "Where will you be comfortable overnight?"

The dragon whuffs amusement. "I doubt you have anywhere large enough to accommodate me. I'll wait here, then at least your people will know where I am and I shan't frighten anyone by appearing unexpectedly."

Princess Rhea raises her eyebrows, as if she wants to say something, then nods. With a flurry of orders I'm packed off to my tent to catch a few hours' sleep and return in the morning with my gear.

But how can I sleep? I just met a *dragon* and I'm going to go with it to meet others. I hope Phoenix finds out.

~ | ~

"You really are a yes-man, Eitel." My sergeant, who also happens to be my cousin, says, shaking his head. "Who were you trying to impress, you idiot? The prince? Or is it that blonde hunk of muscle you've been chasing for weeks?"

"I happen to feel it's my duty," I answer loftily, shoving the last few items into my pack. A blanket, clean stockings and shirt, my spoon, cup and bowl. What did one need to visit dragons?

Would we need to hunt for our own food, or would they fell game for us? Flint, steel and a tiny bundle of kindling, and all the other basics of a Huonese soldier's gear.

"You said that when you enlisted. We both know you were just following me into the army."

You asshole. I look him in the eye. "You got me drunk and told me how great it was!"

He explodes. "I also told you that ice sprites danced under the willow trees at winter solstice when you were eight and you stayed out all night looking for them! You almost died from the cold you caught!"

"Stupid of me to trust my cousin," I shoot back, tightening the straps and hoisting my pack.

He pinches the bridge of his nose, exasperated. "Look, Eitel, that's the problem—you're too trusting. How do you know these dragons aren't just going to eat you! I can't look after you if you go."

Glaring, I make a big show of checking my sword belt buckle, fussing with how the weapons sit. I'd prefer to have the knife on the left instead of the sword, but joining the army meant I had to learn to fight right-handed.

"I don't need you to look after me, Jep." My voice stays low, trying to hide my hurt. *But he always has. All the scrapes you got into, who pulled you out of them?*

Jep sighs. We say nothing more as we march out of the camp, curious eyes following us in the dawn light.

Up in the town, Kyan is surrounded by Medvajan soldiers in the square. While caution still imbues the mist-laden air, I can hear the dragon's rumbling voice and… laughter? Those closest to Kyan's head are chortling like they've just heard a great joke. Jep exchanges a look with me.

"Eitel!" It's the prince. Jep and I straighten, saluting. "Good, you're here. This is Seamus." He gestures to a burly blacksmith, an armorer I've seen at the forge, who nods. I stand a little taller. Forget Phoenix, Seamus is exactly the sort of man I like. Muscles you could crack rocks on, with the seriousness of a scholar. And being the only two Huonese on this mission, we'll no doubt rely on each other. My mind immediately skips to Seamus and I, working the forge, stripping off to bathe afterwards, locking eyes…

"Be courteous. Be diplomatic," Gereon interrupts my thoughts. "You are soldiers of Huon—your duty is to protect." Seamus grunts affirmation and bows. I salute again.

The other volunteers are a farmer, a weaver, a leatherworker, a musician, and of course, Anasta the soldier from last night. All Medvajans, all hiding their nerves with pale faces and grim determination.

They must really trust their princess. Or are they foolhardy like me, trying to prove something? We line up, and Princess Rhea's voice rings out as she looks at us. "You represent our peoples."

Nerves seize me. It's all happening so fast.

Kyan lowers his belly to the ground. Someone has rigged ropes around his neck and belly, presumably to make it easier for us to hold on. The princess continues. "Impress our new allies with your ingenuity and skill. Learn all you can. We will hold the line here in the north, while you forge friendships in the west."

It's a stirring speech, and I feel my chest swell. We clamber onto the dragon's back and as I breathe in the strong, warm scent I catch Jep's eye. Kyan's wings spread. A pit opens in my stomach as my ears fill with the rush of wind.

I wonder what will happen if our trust is misplaced.

Two

Turns out I'm not a great flyer.

We leave the gloomy clouds of the lowlands behind and the sun chases us for hours. When we finally alight in a high mountain valley and shelter from the chill wind, it's pleasant. Or at least it would be if I wasn't vomiting my guts up.

"Worse than a ship," Eveline, the weaver, passes me a waterskin sympathetically.

"What do ye know of ships, Evvy?" Hartleigh, the farmer, is cozy in his thick woolen jacket and felt hat. "Ye've never been on more than a skiff on the river."

Eveline pokes her tongue out. "My cousin is a sailor, and he writes me his adventures."

"Aye, the cousin who'll come back t'marry ye one day, hence why ye keep spurning my advances," he grumbles good-naturedly. "When will ye see there's a good solid man who'll warm ye bed and keep ye well."

"Get away with ye." She flaps her hand and then returns to fussing over me.

"Thank you," I croak, sipping slowly. What I wouldn't give for a cup of Uraidlan green tea to warm and settle my insides.

"Are you well enough to continue?" Kyan returns from the icy stream where he's slaked his own thirst.

"Of course!" I pull myself together. "I don't wish to be the cause for delay."

"Take your time, boy," calls Nyree, the leathermaker, a middle-aged woman who looks as tough as her wares. Her skin, or at least what I can see above the tightly wrapped scarf, is decidedly pale and I'm relieved I'm not the only one who isn't enjoying being airborne.

"He's fine," Anasta snaps. She stalks over and hauls me up by the arm. I'm impressed at her wiry strength—I'm not a small fellow. "You're a soldier," she hisses in my ear. "Act like one."

Seamus eyes me from across the wind-whipped grass, unimpressed. I clear my throat and straighten. Wouldn't want him to think I'm lily-livered. "I'm good to go on." *Glad Jep isn't here to see me like this.*

"I'll speak to one of my fellow mages about a spell or tonic to quell the motion sickness," Kyan declares, curving his neck to watch us as we all climb aboard again, securing ourselves with the ropes. "It will not do for the council to think humans ill-adjusted to flying."

"I don't have bloody wings," I mutter. "Of course I'm ill-adjusted to flying." But what does he mean? He mentioned a council before. Are they the ones we need to impress?

We fly on, and I battle my churning guts miserably, unable to appreciate the spectacular view as we descend into a narrow canyon, shooting out across a wide plateau. A huge expanse of water fills the horizon beyond the cliffs. I've never seen the sea before. It makes me wonder what else is out there.

~ | ~

Kyan lands on a flat, stony riverbank, and solid ground is my friend as I slide off his back. Other dragons whirl closer, growling in excitement, their multi-hued wings filling the air like a rainbow. I should be afraid, but all I can think is at least if they eat us now I won't have to worry about the flight back home. Anasta jabs me with her elbow to stand up straight. I breathe through my nose, glad I have nothing left to vomit.

Guttural exchanges take place between Kyan and the dragons who land nearby. "Doesnae seem like they speak our language," Hartleigh mutters to Eveline as we slide down.

Draconic heads snap around. "I will perform the spell of tongues," Kyan tells us. "It is what I used on myself to speak to

Princess Rhea, but it will be simpler for me to enact it on you so you may understand my kin. May I have your permission?"

We humans exchange bewildered glances.

"I will," I grunt, conscious of redeeming my image amongst them and to Seamus. Kyan smiles, a terrifying sight, but I'm still too nauseated to be scared. He incants, and the air shimmers, then he licks my forehead. Surprised, I stumble back into Anasta, who glares at me.

"Oh, they are too cute!" a nearby dragon says to another excitedly. "I really want one."

"They aren't pets, Axel!" This dragon is black, the first speaker a light green.

"But look, Liuda! Kyan had them riding on him—I could totally carry one about. I wonder what they eat."

"I can understand you!" I rasp.

Draconic heads snap around. My voice doesn't sound like my own, but I know I spoke. This is confirmed when Axel squawks, "It talked! Oh, please can I have one!"

"You may not," Kyan informs them drily. "The humans are here as part of a cultural exchange."

"We know! We heard Kamelya speak to the Council," Liuda retorts. "Grevillus is furious you brought them here. But we think it exciting. And they can speak to us now?"

"What's going on?" Anasta hisses at me.

I blink at her, and at the others huddled behind us. "I can understand them. He did a spell—magic!" I still feel sick but astonishment is flooding me. I'd heard claims of Uraidlan sorceresses that could read your future, and in the Empire mages studied arcane runes to bring about enchantments, but a simple soldier like me never expected to see real magic. Mind you, I never expected to leave Huon—Caelon is the farthest I'd ever been from home, yet today I've flown over the breadth of Medvaja and then across the western mountains.

Anasta nods grimly, then steps up. "Will you perform the spell on me, Lord Kyan?"

"Please, don't call me a lord," the dragon admonishes gently. "Too many outside my wing think I'm conceited as it is. I'm a councilor, and a mage, but we have no lords here."

That shimmer again, and Anasta stares boldly at the other dragons, waiting for them to speak.

"Here comes Kamelya now," Liuda declares and Anasta jerks in surprise. We all look at where the black dragon points.

"They certainly come in all colors," Eveline murmurs. She's huddled near Hartleigh, though not so close as to give him ideas. Seamus is frowning, while Nyree and Shrusti watch nervously as even more wings beat the air. A red dragon—smaller than Kyan but bigger than Axel and Liuda—coasts to join us, two female humans on its back. One of them is waving.

"Anasta!" The taller female, a Medvajan captain by her uniform, leaps off the red dragon's shoulder as soon as she lands. She charges up and clasps the other soldier's arm, then bows to Kyan.

"She agreed?" she demands of him, seemingly oblivious to the fact that he could crush her with barely a thought.

"I told you Kyan would convince her," the red dragon chuckles, lowering herself to the ground so the other rider, a lithe, dark-haired woman, could slide gracefully down.

"She did," Kyan confirms. He raises his voice and addresses everyone in the dragon-tongue. "Tell the others I will address them this evening at the council. Now give our guests some space! You are frightening them."

He seems to be directing his words towards a medium-sized black dragon who is glaring at us with predatory intent.

"You put the whole Weyr at risk, bringing these creatures in," the black dragon criticizes. His amber eyes burn with suspicion.

"You're being paranoid," Kyan snaps. "You'll have your chance to speak at the council. Now go!"

The black dragon sneers, but takes to the air with lethal grace. He soars just over our heads and everyone but me ducks—I'm too in awe of the power in his wings and the whip of his long, sinuous tail. The wind buffets me and I stagger, jaw dropping.

"Never can just do as he's told!" the red dragon hisses.

Axel grumbles as Liuda hustles him away.

"I wanted to pat one!" His voice fades on the breeze.

"Why did they leave?" The tall Medvajan captain frowns. "What did you say?"

Kyan reverts to our human tongue. "I asked them to give us space—there will be a council meeting at dusk, but I need to speak to Kamelya first and see how my proposal was received."

"Ah. Politics." She glances at the other humans. "I am Captain Yatina al Stauberg, of Princess Rhea's Royal Guard. I will be responsible for your safety while you are here, as will Anasta." She narrows her eyes at my uniform. "You are one of Prince Gereon's men?"

I clear my throat. "I am. Eitel Jarvo, infantry."

She nods, relief crossing her face. Glad I'm just a grunt perhaps, rather than an officer who might pull rank on her? Anasta still looks unimpressed.

The others introduce themselves, some boldly, some tentatively. Kyan insists on performing the spell of tongues on them all including Captain al Stauberg and her companion, the very pretty Monique Yulic. Even Hartleigh seems to forget his lovelorn devotion for Eveline and gazes at Mistress Yulic with speculation. Eveline rolls her eyes.

~ | ~

Under Kyan and Kamelya's protective gaze, we rest for several hours as the afternoon sun creeps on. I peek over at Seamus from time to time but he doesn't seem to notice. I can hear Jep in my head, berating me for chasing after a new man so soon, but clearly Phoenix was a mistake, so I might as well make a fresh start.

If you put as much energy into your drills as you do chasing ass, you'd make sergeant! Jep's voice is exasperated. It's a conversation we've had many a time.

But I have you to be my sergeant, Jep. I chuckle to myself. A quiet pang hits me. He's not here to tell me what to do now. *Captain al Stauberg is here to give orders, so I don't have to think too hard, just do as I'm told.*

"Going to eat, soldier boy?" Nyree interrupts my musings. Cold water from the river has settled my nausea.

"Thanks." I accept the roll she passes over. Stuffed with almonds and apricot pieces, I chew and sigh contentedly.

"Who would have thought yesterday we would be on the other side of the mountains, meeting dragons?" I wave my half-eaten roll. "What an adventure!"

Seamus overhears, and gives me an incredulous look. Shrusti is humming, occasionally mouthing a few words as she taps a beat only she can hear. Now that I don't feel sick, I can observe my companions. Anasta shadows Captain al Stauberg, as stern as Seamus is dour. I give him another sidelong glance. He ignores me. That's alright—I'm used to his type playing hard to get.

Hartleigh questions Monique about how she came to be here.

"I met Kamelya and some of the other dragons several times in the last few months, during the Exchange," she tells him. "I've been sketching and painting for the court, but she wanted some paintings of her own." She smiles up at the red dragon, who speaks intently to Kyan and the captain, just out of earshot. "I'm glad this alliance isn't just relying on my artwork—I understand you all have skills to show the Weyr?"

"Well, I'm a farmer," Hartleigh begins, "so I'm not sure how I'll put that on display, but I can talk to them about the kinds of crops I grow." He deflates as he goes on. "But I don't suppose they have a need for oats or barley."

"Aye, they probably eat meat," Seamus mutters.

We all pause. "Well, we haven't been eaten yet," I say cheerfully. "Seems like a good start!" Seamus glares at me. *He really leans into the stoic, grumpy smith persona, doesn't he?*

I shrug. He'll warm up to me. They usually do.

~ | ~

As the sun dips towards the horizon, several dragons return to take us to a great stone amphitheater downriver of where we rested. Axel begs to be allowed to carry one of us, so I'm clinging to his neck ridges, back to wanting to vomit as we descend jerkily. As soon as we land, I slide down and hit the ground with relief. Axel turns back to me and beams.

"I hope you'll be allowed to stay in my weyr!" he exclaims.

Liuda lands more gracefully beside him and shakes her head, Shrusti on her back. "I don't think he's well, Axel, perhaps you should take him to Callistemon after this. She's good with animals."

"Not an animal," I mutter, though I don't think they hear me. I drag myself to attention as Kamelya lands and Captain al Stauberg strides to the fore.

We stand in the center of the amphitheater, huge carved rock steps rising in rings, the top-most rung several dragon-lengths above our heads. It's too regular to be natural, though for the life of me I cannot fathom how it was carved, particularly since the river curves around its southern side. It would have taken a team of thousands to mason away at the granite—are dragon claws so strong?

On each row perches dozens of dragons of varying sizes and colors. Some are smaller than Axel. One giant black creature is joined by Kamelya and Kyan. Necks crane and comments fly until a large gold dragon swings its tail against a huge gong that hangs from a stone arch. The sound reverberates through my teeth, and I see Monique flinch.

"Order!" The gold dragon commands. "The council is now in session. Kyan of the Malachite Clan, you may speak."

Kyan inclines his head. "Thank you, Councilor Iqbal." He takes a deep breath. "Council members, clans-folk and wing-kin, I bring before you representatives of the human kingdoms to the east, who wish to befriend dragonkind and further the alliance which I brokered last summer. You all know my belief that friendship between our realms is of benefit to us both, and from the initial trust we have built, this courageous group comes to share skills and other aspects of their own culture, so that we may learn from them, and know our similarities as civilized, thinking beings."

A mutter of dissension arises from a blue dragon, and it's only then I notice that aside from those grouped at Kyan's side, the council is divided by color. Behind the grumbling blue, the tiers are crowded with dragons whose scales vary from the palest blue to the darkest navy. To their left, split by no discernable marker, sit browns, oranges, tans, and even a couple that can only be described as sepia.

Greens are next, from muddy olive to bright emerald, then purples, then shades of yellows. Blacks and greys are followed by reds, then chalky whites. Kyan's group sit between the whites and the blues, upsetting the homogeny of the color wheel. I don't know what to make of it.

"Councilor Kyan's views are well-known," the dark blue dragon drawls. "He is to be praised for his success in protecting our young from human hunting, but the mountains serve as a natural barrier, and it seems folly to broach that with additional contam… contact."

Anasta bristles, but Captain al Stauberg quells her with a look and squares her shoulders. "May I address the council, honored people?" Her voice rings out, no doubt used to a parade ground.

A stir of astonishment ripples through the assembled dragons. "She speaks our tongue!" a yellow dragon hisses.

"Kyan!" demands another. "What have you done?"

Kyan is unmoved. "It seemed expedient that we speak directly, unimpeded by translation. This way, we may communicate without confusion."

"Order!" The gold dragon, Councilor Iqbal, slams the gong again. "Kyan, explain yourself."

"I have, honored councilor." Kyan cocks his head. "This council gave me leave to stop the hunting and deaths of our young by whatever means necessary. I chose diplomacy over violence, and continue to choose it to the benefit of our kind. An alliance with these humans is important, and you all know why."

Discontented murmurs break out, until Iqbal barks again for order. He glares at everyone, then turns to Captain al Stauberg. "Very well. Human, you may speak."

The captain seems to choose her words carefully. "Honored dragons, my name is Captain Yatina al Stauberg. My princess sent us here to further the bonds of alliance into friendship. She, herself, cannot attend because she defends her northern border from an enemy kingdom, and will not leave her people without protection. But she entrusts me to speak on her behalf." She takes a deep breath. "Here with me stand folk from my land, Medvaja, and our ally to the east, Huon, to share culture and learnings, so dragonkind might understand us better."

The blue dragon looks as if a rat has crawled under its nose and died. A black dragon glares with vehemence. *Is that the same one from earlier?* I can't tell, but I think it is. He's lean compared to the stocky grey next to him, and twitches with suspicious agitation.

Others dragons, however, look curious, and Councilor Iqbal sighs. "Would any of the council like to ask the humans questions?"

"What culture?" shoots the ruby-scaled dragon to our left. "We've seen the paintings. Have you more of those?"

"Paintings are pretty but not useful," an olive creature on the opposite side says.

"Don't be such a boor, Nyssa," a mauve dragon chides from behind me. I swing my head to look, and a toothy grin meets my gaze. "Well, humans, what else can you do?"

Nyree clears her throat, and shoots me a look of fear. I smile at her encouragingly. "I…" she squeaks and clears her throat again. "I'm a leather maker. Harnesses and jerkins and suchlike."

"What did it say?"

"It? She's a female, can't you scent that, you belly-crawler? I swear your egg was dropped."

The bickering is cut off by Iqbal booming. "This female is a leather maker."

Seamus clears his throat. "I'm a smith," he intones. "Mostly weapons, since I'm in the army, but tools, horseshoes…" He looks around and seems to realize shoeing horses would scarcely be of interest to a cavern of dragons. "I can do jewelry, metal ornaments, chains—decorative or functional." His self-assurance stirs me—ancestors know I love a confident man.

"I'm a weaver," Eveline speaks up. "Mostly wool, some hemp. Flax from the south if I can get it."

"You weave… plants?" a yellow dragon asks.

"Could be useful for baskets, I suppose," the olive dragon says doubtfully.

"Clothes!" Hartleigh steps up. "She weaves fabric to make clothes, and blankets, and bags and more. She is very skilled!"

Eveline shoots him a sardonic look. "And Hartleigh here is a farmer. He grows crops and raises cattle, pigs, chickens and geese."

That catches the attention of most of the group.

"We have been rude, and not asked your names," the mauve dragon smiles. "I am Gyeltshen, of Amethyst Clan."

From then on each dragon gives its name before it speaks, and we give our names in turn. Dark blue Muscario of Sapphire Clan, does so reluctantly, and after Anasta and I introduce ourselves he mutters, "They send soldiers into our midst."

The council appears divided on whether our presence is for good or ill, but a vote passes that we are to spend time with a host and they can question us while we demonstrate our skills. This leads to another shouting match and I can tell Nyree is trying not to cower. Hartleigh puts an arm about Eveline but she shakes him off. Captain al Stauberg looks worriedly at Monique, who has pursed lips.

"Enough!" Iqbal strikes the gong again. I can see Seamus eyeing the great bronze disc with interest.

"We'll take the musician, Shrusti," Gyeltshen declares.

"The male who works with metal." This is from a great brown dragon.

"The leather maker," volunteers a buttery yellow dragon.

"The farmer," from the greens.

"The female soldier," grins a red.

"The weaver." Muscario eyes Eveline, who swallows.

Heads turn between the remaining two groups. A chalky pale dragon shrugs. "The artist will do. A librarian would have been better. Do you have such things as libraries, humans? Books?"

"We do," Monique curtsies gracefully. "I also speak several languages other than Medvajan, so perhaps we can discuss translation."

This perks the white dragon up, and I look hesitantly to the dark greys and blacks. "Then you are with us," the stocky grey dragon sighs with distaste. "I am Grevillus."

I glance at Kyan, trying to hide my trepidation. Grevillus does not seem enthused about hosting me. Unfortunately, Kyan is deep in discussion with Kamelya.

I swallow, looking back at Grevillus, then straighten my shoulders. He jerks his head towards the still-glaring black dragon beside him.

"Damir, bring him back to Obsidian Weyr."

Three

"Are they meant to change color like this? Oh dear, what's coming out of its mouth? That's rather disgusting."

I can barely hear them—flight-sickness hits me hard again and chunks of apricot barely miss a wing as the dragon places me on the ground. It would appear that dangling from a set of talons is worse than riding on a dragon's back, and Damir can't let go of me fast enough once I start spewing.

"Get Callistemon—she surely has some herb or tincture that might help."

"Urgh." I want to die. Unable to move, I listen distantly until a pungent scent wafts up my nostrils and adrenaline has me coursing upright. "Ancestors!" I choke. "What is that?"

"Hmm, possibly an even smaller dose. Hard to know, given the size." An unfamiliar dragon hazes into view. She has a distinctly feminine voice, scales the color of a burnt sunset and... broken wings. I blink.

"Can you walk, human?" she asks.

"Uhh, I think so." Sitting in a puddle of my own bile, I look around. We're in a cave entrance, with a couple of grey and black dragons watching from just outside.

"Then come," the orange dragon instructs. She turns and paces into a side tunnel.

Shambling after her, it takes me a few moments to realize what is wrong with her back. A twisted ruin emerges where her wings should be. I'm mesmerized but hold my tongue. She's still thirty feet long and could bite me in half, or simply squash me.

Years of having manners beaten into me and Jep yelling orders have taught me when to keep my trap shut.

We descend to a lower level, reaching a cave lit by strange crystals embedded in the walls. It's humid down here. I sniff—the faint odor of rotten eggs permeates the damp air.

The orange dragon halts at a workbench as tall as me. Plants and fungi grow in wall recesses, unfazed by the lack of sunlight. Clay bowls and jars line the stone shelves and on the workbench are mortar and pestle.

She puts down the covered bowl she has been carrying and considers me. Her expression is... sympathetic?

"They said Councilor Kyan had brought a party of humans to the Weyr. After hearing all the stories, I expected you to be... more fearsome."

"I *am* a soldier." A pretty pathetic one right now, though. Jep would have disowned me. *He'd know what to do, though.*

"A soldier? A fighter? Whom do you fight?"

She's got a point. My weapons are with our packs—where did they even end up? All I carry is a knife in my belt, and my physical strength, while handy in a brawl or skirmish, is useless here, even against a... crippled dragon?

My eyes must give me away, because she chuckles. "I suppose I'm not what you expected either. My wings did not grow in the shell as they should. Dragons like me usually don't survive." She chuckles again. "But I'm tenacious. And my mind is sharper than most."

I nod slowly. "Forgive me. What should I call you?"

She smiles toothily. "Callistemon. Originally of Axinite Clan, but I dwell with Obsidian now. And you are?"

"Eitel Jarvo, soldier of Huon." Looking around at the plants, the jars, the tools. "Or just Eitel. You're an apothecist."

Her grin broadens. "You're observant. You have such as me in your lands."

I nod. "Have you got anywhere I can clean up, my lady? I have no idea where my pack is, but I'd like to wash the vomit from my shirt." Perhaps one of those bowls holds water.

She laughs. "Just Callistemon will do. I am not your female. And yes, there is a bathing pool through that arch. I cannot fly to the river like the others."

Cheered by the prospect of getting clean, I follow her directions and discover a stunning underground pool.

Luminescence turns the water an eerie green but I'm just glad it's not dark. Stripping off my jerkin and shirt, I'm relieved to see it's only the sleeves that I've spattered. *Don't want Seamus to know I threw up.*

Bracing myself for the cold, I dip a hand in the pool and exclaim.

"Is something wrong, little human?" Callistemon calls.

"I didn't expect it to be warm!"

Her amused face appears in the archway. "Warm water is much better for my muscles. My condition is such that I ache every day."

"Oh." I avert my gaze.

"I'm not diseased." Her tone takes on a sharp edge. "You cannot catch my affliction."

Horrified, I raise my eyes to hers. "I didn't mean that! It's just… you're right, meeting so many dragons today and I don't want to give offence!"

She softens. "Feel free to bathe, Eitel. I imagine this is bewildering, and you have been separated from your companions. Bathe, sleep and no doubt Grevillus and the others will have questions for you tomorrow."

~ | ~

I don't need to be told twice. After weeks on the march from Huon to Caelon, then the onset of rain, not to mention a freezing flight from one side of the mountain range to the other… and here I am getting a hot bath. Things are definitely looking up, bewildering dragons or not.

I wash my shirt and stockings, scrubbing them against the rock and laying them on a ledge. Then, completely naked, I immerse myself in the water.

I groan with pleasure as I discover the pool's heat emanates from an upwelling in the center. I stay near the edge to avoid boiling myself, but I imagine a dragon would find it delightful.

I haven't been this clean in an age. I use my knife to trim my nails and effect a rough shave, then I sigh with satisfaction as I relax into the heat and let my mind wander.

I hope the others are getting the royal treatment too. The thought of Seamus, his hard, muscled form slipping into a hot pool like this has my hand circling my cock and giving it an idle stroke. I close my eyes and envision Seamus' strong hands turning me around to face the wall of the pool. I keep working myself slowly, adding a languorous twist into each stroke.

Seamus, slipping a finger down to tease my ass. Seamus, not saying a word but just opening me up, gently but persistent. Seamus, the round knob of his cock nudging at my entrance.

My hand moves faster, the hot water a delicious swirl around my shaft. I tease just under the knob, envisioning Seamus pushing into me, inch at a time. I know he'll fill me, touch that part inside me that makes me see stars. My breath comes faster.

I hear movement. I whirl in the water to face Callistemon, hand automatically reaching for a sword that isn't there.

But it's not her. It's Damir. She might be smaller than him but she is slow and deliberate while he is lithe and sinuous. Her manner relaxes my guard, his puts it straight back up again.

"Callistemon, why is this creature in your bathing pool?" He sounds appalled. I hasten to answer.

"Uhh, she said I could clean up in here." I feel far more heat in my face than can be explained by the pool. *Do dragons blush? Probably not.*

She appears behind him. "You made me responsible for him tonight, and he wished to bathe." She doesn't sound… worried, but she's not as mild as before.

"How do you know it won't contaminate the water?" Damir's lip curls. "It should get out."

I hold up my hands, mortified that I was close to climaxing in the pool and they might consider that contamination. "I can get out." I'm not hugely fond of the idea of being stark naked and still hard in front of two dragons but if it deescalates the situation, I'm all for it. Hoisting myself out of the pool, I inch towards my trousers.

"It's Eitel, by the way." I keep my voice calm, although my hands are itching for a spear or even my stupid army-issued short-sword. "You're Damir, right?"

His lip curls further. *Guess we're not on first name terms yet.*

"And what is that?" he demands.

Oh. Thank the ancestors the pool was warm, or I'd be even more embarrassed.

"Damir, even on a human, surely you can work that out," Callistemon barely reins in her exasperation. "You've assisted me enough times with injured animals."

I clear my throat and bend slowly for my trousers. "I don't wish to give offence. Just let me cover up."

"Cover up! Can you not retract it? Or are you aroused?" The black dragon sounds outraged.

"No!" *Not anymore.* Struggling to maintain dignity, I thrust one leg then the other into my trousers and lace up, feeling somehow more protected despite the fact that cloth and leather will do nothing to stop this dragon chomping me into pieces. "It's not retractable."

He leans forward and sniffs me deeply. I suppress hysterical laughter as I'm reminded of a guard hound deciding whether or not to pounce on an intruder.

"No," he concludes. "You're not aroused at this time."

"Uhh, you can smell that?" *Ancestors, what did he smell when he first came in?*

How I've come to interpret draconic expressions so quickly is beyond me, but there's no doubt the look he throws me is withering.

"Damir, enough." Callistemon nudges his flank. "You asked me to take care of him for the night. Besides, he wasn't well. This is my weyr and I do as I please."

"Hmph, well he seemed diseased."

"It was the flying!" I protest. "I felt sick from all the jolting around."

Damir snorts in disgust. "And they expect us to treat them as people. They are nothing but animals."

"Hold up!" I clench my fists. "I've never flown before, at least I had the decency not to vomit all over you!"

Aaaand, he's definitely going to eat you now. I can see Jep in my mind, closing his eyes in resignation as I shoot my mouth off.

Damir's eyes widen, then he whirls and barges past Callistemon, his tail almost whipping me in the process. I am left, still dripping and half-naked, while the orange dragon considers me inscrutably.

I clear my throat. "My apologies for raising my voice in your home, Lady Callistemon."

A slow grin spreads across her face. "Call me Calli, Eitel. Forgive Damir's rudeness—he has always been over-protective. Join me when you're ready, and I'll have something for you to eat. I also can make a tonic to help your airsickness. You will probably be doing a lot of flying while you're in the Weyr."

Four

Callistemon weighs me in a huge set of scales that sits at the end of her giant workbench. I'm still embarrassed about the confrontation earlier, and sitting in the scales makes me feel like a child—something a large man like me doesn't experience often. I don't know what to say, and no one is here to tell me how to act, so I remain uncomfortably silent.

After weighing me, she crushes several odious-smelling roots and steeps them in a cauldron of boiling water. I'm glad of the fire in the hearth, though it's not wood that burns but strange black rocks. The cave would be chilly without the heat, and I'm able to dry my shirt and stockings. She grills fish over the fire too, and I gratefully eat.

"You can drink this in the morning." She indicates the bubbling liquid in the cauldron. "I use a similar concoction to alleviate queasiness in dragons and animals alike."

"Thank you…" I pause, then decide not to comment. Damir's comments about me being an animal rankle, and I'm sure he's not the only dragon to think so. I wish Jep or even Captain al Stauberg were here to tell me what to say. I didn't expect to be on my own when I volunteered. Now I'm very conscious that I'm not equipped to deal with this diplomatic palaver.

"You can make a nest in here, since it's warmer. I sleep in that nook, so if you get scared, just know I'll be nearby." She pauses. "The privy is through the bathing cave. Throw ash from the bowl in afterwards please."

I glance back through the archway. "It's a little dark." I'm embarrassed to sound like a coward but I also don't want to break my leg.

"Is it?" She cocks her head. "Do humans need more light to see?"

"Uh, I suppose? Is it not dark for you?" I finish the fish, glad to be feeling full and not queasy again. After using the privy, I will gladly fall asleep. No point worrying about tomorrow until it comes.

"No." Callistemon considered. "Use this." She removes a small gem from a clay jar and taps it with a claw. It lights up, a soft yellow glow that is stronger than a candle yet without the flicker. I gasp.

"How does it work?" *There's no flame!*

She shrugs. "The student mages spell them. Very useful for the deeper caves, where no moonlight or starlight reaches, or for my plants." She gestures to several more gems embedded into the ceiling, and I realize the fire is not the only source of light in the cave.

"Incredible! That must be so useful."

"It needs to be respelled from time to time, but it shouldn't burn you, I would think." Placing it down on the ground next to where I sit cross-legged, I notice again how carefully and deliberately she moves. Damir had barreled in and at the council the other dragons had filled the space more assertively. Callistemon is judicious in her actions, expending no excess energy, it would seem.

I touch the glowing gem. It is warm, but not hot. "Thank you," I say. "And for the meal, and the bath too. I haven't felt this human in weeks."

She chuckles, sitting back. "What an odd saying. What do you mean?"

"Uhh…" I suppress a belch. "Just being clean and warm and fed does wonders for the soul, I guess. My country is at war, so is Medvaja, so I've been on the front, sleeping in wet and muddy camps and running patrols through the hills." I feel a pang of guilt, wondering how Jep and my comrades are.

"Hmm."

Later, stretched out under my cloak on a bearskin fur, I listen to Callistemon's steady breathing. I'm too contented and warm to stay awake long. I drift off, imagining everyone else in their own warm nests. *I wonder if Seamus snores.*

~ | ~

"Absolutely freezing to bathe in…"

"… glad we brought blankets…

"…put me in a pen! Like a dog!"

"Pass me that, I'm so hungry. They had water in the cave but no food!"

"It's called a weyr, and I'll speak to Kyan about making sure they supply food before we go." Kamelya exchanges an exasperated look with Captain al Stauberg.

"Kamelya, are they going to be treated alright?" the captain asks in a low voice, not noticing that I'd sidled closer. "This could be a disaster."

"It'll be fine. Kyan will check on everyone while Doru and I are gone."

The captain doesn't look convinced, but relief fills her face as a white dragon alights and Monique slides gracefully down. "Are you alright?" She embraces Monique, kissing her forehead.

"Fine," the dark haired woman smiles. "Amanita was a most gracious host and I made sure she knew what I needed."

"Oh, really?" Kamelya swings her head around and sniffs Monique, then the white dragon, and harumphs. "I suppose."

"I don't see why she couldn't have stayed with us in your weyr again," the captain grumbles.

"It will be well, Yatina," Monique strokes the captain's cheek. "We must all do our part."

We are by the river again, in the center of the valley, and the cool, fresh air is invigorating after the warmth of Callistemon's cave. Grevillus asked a number of questions this morning about what I did as a soldier. I described the drills and training we do. He listened carefully but some of the other dragons were clearly bored and wandered off—disappearing into caves or flying out of the huge, bowl-shaped recess that seems to be Obsidian Clan's central gathering area. Damir stared at me unnervingly the whole time, then curled his lip when Grevillus ordered him to bring me to the river, but at least he didn't drop me.

We've regrouped for a mid-morning meal. Now that I think of it, we've also regrouped to check that everyone is still alive.

"You haven't said much, Eitel." Nyree is skinning a deer. A bright yellow dragon caught it this morning for her, she said. She works the knife steadily, pulling the hide away to reveal bright red muscles. Hartleigh and Anasta gather firewood in the scrubby bushes nearby, and I'm gathering nice round stones from the river to construct a cooking pit. The dried meat strips Kamelya brought have not been enough to sustain us all and a proper meal is required before we split up again.

"Nothing much to say," I grunt as I haul up a flat rock that will serve well to prepare food on. I don't know if we'll be meeting here every day, out in the open air, but at least there is none of the rain that plagues east of the mountains at this time of year. Besides, it doesn't hurt to show off to Seamus how strong I am. "My host's name is Callistemon. Seems to be some kind of apothecist or physician. She gave me this tonic that's cured my flight-sickness."

It was true—the short flight in Damir's claws didn't upset me in the slightest. I'm hoping longer flights will be the same.

"An apothecist?" Seamus appears and rearranges the stones of my cooking pit. I hide my annoyance but let him. "Seems incredible they have such things."

"They have crystals that glow—better than lanterns or candles," I inform him, hoping to impress with my knowledge.

"Aye, I saw those." He nods. "Would be useful in the forge since they don't have the heat."

"Do you think they'll want to eat the scraps?" Nyree whispers to me as she saws off the deer's head. Blood splatters her cheek but she's also wearing yesterday's dirt still.

"I can ask." I take the head. "Did they have a bathing pool where you were?"

Her eyebrow's furrow. "Not that I saw."

A shadow passes overhead and Kyan circles to land, Axel and Liuda trailing in his wake. They clutch our packs in their claws.

"Alright, whose is this?" Axel raises my pack and gives it a shake. "I'm on delivery duty, so I'll take it to your host clan's weyr. Apparently you need to be fed more frequently so Liuda and I will hunt this evening as well."

"That one's mine." I raise my bloody hand, other one still holding the head of the deer. "Will you eat this?"

"I will." Liuda's jaws snake forward faster than I can see and snatch the deer head from my fingers. She tosses it in the air, sears it with a burst of flame from her maw and crunches it down.

My jaw hangs open, as do the jaws of those around me.

"Show off," grumbles Axel.

Liuda smiles smugly. "Just because you haven't mastered the fire spell."

"You can work on the ice spell next, then." Kyan's rumble is stern. "Now make yourself useful and help Axel deliver our guests' belongings."

"Did ye see that?" Seamus whispers. He's pale under his tan.

"Handy for lighting the forge." Strangely, I'm not frightened like everyone else seems to be. *That's because it takes someone with a brain to be frightened!* I can hear Jep say. I grimace, eyeing the cooking pit. *My set up was perfectly fine, Seamus didn't have to go changing it.* But men like him don't like being challenged, I've always found, not if I want to have any hope of getting him into bed.

You never have a problem getting them into bed, just keeping them around afterwards. I brush off the thoughts and smile at Seamus. He frowns back at me.

Maybe I should try being more assertive, and see what happens.

~ | ~

Captain al Stauberg speaks with each of us in turn, Kyan interjecting with questions, before we return to our respective weyrs. When I report on my host situation, the others exclaim about the hot pool.

"I told you Callistemon is good with… she's good with everyone." Liuda corrects herself when Kyan, much larger than her, swings his head around in warning.

"I get it," I say. "You think we're animals, and I'd hazard a lot of humans think dragons are animals. Isn't that the whole point of this envoy? To overcome that belief on both sides?" *I'm not the sharpest sword in the sheath but surely that's obvious to everyone?*

Monique coughs with amusement, and even the captain hides a grin. Everyone else in earshot shuffles uncomfortably, dragon and human alike.

"You're a foot soldier?" Captain al Stauberg asks. I salute. She mutters, "huh," under her breath and turns to Kyan.

"Will it cause offense if we inspect where everyone is staying? We can't have them putting Eveline in a pen again."

"Agreed," he intones. "I'll be speaking to Muscario directly. We'll go there first."

The other dragons return and collect their various humans. Axel and Liuda have disappeared to hunt in the valleys surrounding the great Weyr, and Kamelya flew east hours before with a huge black dragon whose name I didn't catch.

I'm left waiting for Damir. I tidy the area, using water from the river to wash down the blood from the deer with my wooden cup. After finishing, I sit, sipping water. *An ale would be nice right about now.* It's odd, not having any duties or orders. I let my eyes and mind wander.

Now that I'm not dealing with constant nausea, I can appreciate the view. The plateau upon which the dragons live is not flat. Several miles wide, it's pocked with rocky divots, patches of scrub and copses of trees that cluster near the winding river. Steep cliffs rise to our north, east and south, with only the western coastline dropping away. I wouldn't mind getting a closer look, but it would probably take best part of an hour to reach it and I was told to wait.

So I wait.

Have the Obsidian's forgotten me? I see a shape winging its way towards me. It's black, but instead of relief, nerves pool in my stomach as Damir approaches. He lands, far too close for my liking and grins. He is all teeth, none of it friendly.

"All alone, human?"

Five

To hell with this. It's already clear he doesn't like me, or possibly any human, so I've nothing to lose. "I've been waiting awhile. Are you taking me back to Callistemon?" My voice is nowhere near as firm as I'd like.

"Callistemon's too busy to look after you today."

"Ah." *Look after?* It's basic training all over again, only instead of a cantankerous sergeant, I have a dragon as big as a cottage convinced I need constant supervision. "Grevillus doesn't have any other questions for me? Maybe you could take me to assist Seamus?" I perk up.

Damir cocks his head, nostrils flaring. Without warning he snatches me in one hand and my pack in another, and we launch.

Even without the nausea, my stomach protests as it's left far below. We soar into the sky, following the curve of the river back towards the canyon from which it emerges, away from the coast. The steep mountain that spears up from the canyon's northern wall has a huge chunk missing from its side, a bowl-shaped depression dotted with cave openings all around the rim. Dragons of brown and orange dominate, whether in the air, perched on outcrops or splashing in the lake that fills the lowest part of the bowl. Other colors are present, but it's clear to me that this is the Axinite Clan's weyr. I wonder why Callistemon doesn't live here.

Damir banks and angles for a cluster of boulders. He lands atop one and dangles me down, dropping me the last few feet, my pack thudding beside me. I avoid rolling my ankle only thanks to my army boots, and glare up at him without thinking.

"Could have been a bit gentler!"

His dark, draconic head leans down and a growl reverberates through my bowels. Self-preservation kicks in and I lower my gaze, kneeling to pick up my pack instead. *Maybe if I've got this on he won't want to eat me and get all the leather and fabric stuck in his teeth,* I think hysterically.

"Why is there another one, Damir?" a tired voice asks from above my head. A light tan dragon peers over another boulder.

"Thought he could help with the metal-worker." Damir jerks his head towards the noise coming from behind the grey dragon, a rhythmic clanking and hammering that I recognize instantly.

"Very well." The tan disappears and I hesitate, then follow, edging around the boulder. I glance back at Damir, whose lip curls a fraction. Deciding to put space between myself and him, I hasten to find Seamus.

The big smith is hammering a short length of steel. An open fire blazes beside him, to which he returns the steel for more heating. Liuda crouches nearby, and breathes fire ever so carefully, turning the metal red hot. A dozen dragons cluster around, watching intently.

How can I make myself useful? There's a heavy stone basin of water ready for quenching, and clearly no need to pump bellows.

It's not a sword, or even a knife that Seamus is making. He has several short pieces which he heats, then rounds on the bick of the anvil, which he must have brought with him, along with the tools and metal. Piece by piece, Seamus rounds steel into links of chain, joining two with a third, which he quenches then sets aside. He heats more short pieces, rounds them, and we all watch, mesmerized, as he joins two lengths of three with an additional link to make a chain of seven.

He clears his throat. "Can make a chain as long as ye like, stronger than rope. Doesnae have to be steel. Jewelers use gold and silver and copper and suchlike for necklaces and whatnot." He shoots a wary glance at Liuda. "Human forges take longer to heat and lotta fuel to keep hot."

She smiles. "Pleasure to be of assistance."

"Seamus!" I call out. "Do you need a hand?"

His head whips around, gripping his hammer like a weapon. Clearly he hadn't realized I was there. "Eitel." His mouth twists into a frown. "Don't need yer help." He turns his back to me and picks up a thicker piece. "I'll make a knife."

Deflated, I stand and watch, admiring his skill but put off by his rudeness.

"That human doesn't want you here," murmurs a low voice by my ear. I start—Damir had slunk up silently. *Or was I just too absorbed to notice? Jep would tear strips off me for not paying attention.*

Hiding my mortification, I give the dragon a tight smile and say, "I suppose you're right."

"Come." He jerks his head and returns the way we came, to the other side of the huge boulder. He reaches for me.

"Oh no!" I step back. "Where are you taking me now?"

The ridges above his cat-like eyes rise. I cross my arms.

"If you struggle, I'm more likely to drop you."

"Just ask before you pick me up! Why can't I ride on your back, anyway?"

He peers at me in consternation, then snatches me in his claws before I have the chance to dodge.

"Hey!" I yell. I don't dare squirm because he's right—struggling is likely to end up with me slipping from my pack straps and being lacerated by razor sharp claws if Damir was to try to catch me. He might just let me fall.

I fall silent as I take in the Weyr below. While dragons are visible in the air and on the ground in every direction, the clusters of colors are noticeable in places all around the edge. I can't see any humans at this distance, especially with the wind tearing up my eyes. I can only assume everyone else is with their assigned clan. *Conducting their little demonstrations.*

Damir avoids any centers of activity—we cross the coastline and bank south. *Is he going to drop me in the ocean?* I'm treated to a spectacular view of the river cascading over the cliffs into the sea. White spray creates rainbows as the waves mingle in a mist above dark rocks. The water looks deep and unforgiving—even if my pack didn't tangle me into a watery grave, I'd be dashed against the cliffs if I managed to swim to shore.

Still, Damir doesn't seem incline to drop me yet. He makes for several lumpy islands that rise from greener water—we coast over a small bay and land on a grey sand beach. He even waits until my boots almost touch before letting go. I still lose my footing and land on my ass, my pack breaking some of my fall. Tiny red crabs scuttle away into their burrows.

Groaning, I shrug out of it and get to my feet, inhaling the salty air—nothing like the fields and forests of home. Looking back towards the mainland, I know I'm completely dependent on the goodwill of the dragon who brought me here, unless Kyan or someone decides to come rescue me.

Despite that, my stupid mouth opens and says, "You know, if you wanted to get me alone, you only had to ask."

Damir rears back as if stung. Then he leans in close and sniffs me. "Why do you seek the company of a male who doesn't want you? You desire him, that much is plain. But he does not desire you."

My face flushes. "What do you mean, that much is plain? You don't know me."

The dragon huffs. "I can smell it."

I remember him sniffing me after my bath in Callistemon's cave. "Oh. Right."

"So why?"

I shrug unhappily. "I didn't know he wasn't interested. I just wanted to get to know him." *Seems to be my luck, always picking the wrong men.* I kick the sand. I'm sure tales I've heard told of beaches say the sand is white, or yellow even. *'Ere lie the golden sands of bright Jungshi, from whence sail ships o'er shimmering sea...* Something like that. "Why is the sand here grey?"

Damir looks at the sand, then at me. "Why are you not afraid? The other humans have been, even Kamelya's little pets."

I scratch my head. "My cousin always said I was too stupid to be afraid."

"Ha!"

I'm astonished. I've made him laugh. I give a bashful shrug this time. "Probably I am. It's why I'm better having someone like Jep giving me orders. He got the brains in the family."

A frowning dragon is a terrible sight to behold, but for some reason it makes me laugh in turn.

"Are all humans so dismissive of themselves?" he demands, his tail lashing showers of sand onto the rocks. Seagulls squawk and flutter out of range.

I start to shrug again, then stop before he thinks all humans have a bizarre shoulder twitch. Instead I open my hands out wide. "Can't say. This is the farthest I've ever been from home—a few months ago I didn't really believe dragons existed. Here I am talking with you on an island in a sea that doesn't show on any map I've ever seen."

Damir shuffles so his claws burrow into the sand. "Didn't believe dragons existed?" He's incredulous.

I mimic his relaxed state and sit down, leaning against my pack. The sand is cool under me, with a softness that caresses my hands as I run my fingers through it. "There are no dragons in Huon, or Uraidla, as far as I know. A lot of us thought that tales from Medvaja were just that—tales."

He peppers questions about Huon, and how it differs from the countries surrounding it. I had thought the war with Trevault had been explained to the dragons, but perhaps he hadn't been present for that council. His suspicious manner eases as I keep giving him answers, and I wonder if it was ignorance that had him so wary to begin with.

Speaking of ignorance, I have questions of my own.

"Are there no other realms of dragons?" I ask as the sun bakes down. We don't seem to be going anywhere in a hurry so I shed my jacket and jerkin, taking off my boots to enjoy scrunching my toes in the sand. The water looks inviting—small waves, not the crashing monsters we flew over earlier.

"Are you wishing to bathe?" he asks abruptly, disregarding my question.

An adventurous crab runs across my foot. It tickles. "Is it cold?"

"Dive in and find out." As if in challenge, he marches down the beach into the water, barreling through the small waves and disappearing under the surface. He reappears two dozen yards out, fanning his wings and using them to float atop the gentle swell.

My shirt and pants are off before I think about whether it's a good idea or not. This dragon has already seen me naked, so what of it? I run into the sea and gasp—it's not so cold that I would run straight out again, but it's certainly refreshing. *And then give him another reason to despise humans.*

I'm a strong swimmer—Jep and I often played in Lake Sobhi during hot summers. We would dare each other to swim out the farthest, braving the weeds full of pike and eels to reach the deep water. But where the lake was calm, the sea is alive and keeps smacking me in the face with briny splashes.

"Do all dragons swim?" I call, sculling near Damir.

His eyes fly open. "Do all humans?" If he's impressed at me joining him, he doesn't show it.

"No, not all." I tread water. "I learned as a child."

He drifts closer. "Many dragons enjoy swimming, but not all."

Callistemon, I think. With her crippled wings she wouldn't be able to float the way he does.

I paddle about, deciding not to bother him with questions. The rise and fall of the water is relaxing. Only a madman, or mad dragon, would swim near the cliffs, but here, at this beach, it's delightful.

Eventually I start to chill, so head shoreward. It's harder than I think it should be—we've drifted out into the bay. I persevere. It's tiring, and a sneaky wave cops me in the face, leaving me spluttering. Tightness grips my chest. Is the shore actually getting any closer? *Where is Damir?* I can't see him.

A warm, scaly neck rises under my arm. "Hold on," Damir orders gruffly, emerging from the water. I cling to the spines as his tail propels us back to the beach. It takes long enough even at his swimming speed that I know I would have been in real trouble had he not come to my aid. When I finally stagger out of the shallows I shiver in relief.

"Thank you," I cough, kneeling in the sand. "I didn't realize I'd swum that far."

He nudges me with his snout. "You didn't. There was a current. Could you not feel it?"

I shake my head, shivering in embarrassment.

He huffs. "Cold? Humans are so poorly regulated. Is that why you wear extra skins?" He breathes warm air on me. I sigh as my strength returns.

"That and modesty." I half-gesture between my legs, not really wanting to draw attention but illustrating the point.

He does the opposite of what I hope. Instead of taking the hint and giving me privacy, he thrusts his snout closer and sniffs. "Why is it so much smaller than last night?" he demands.

I cover my cock with my hands. "Alright, ease up, it's cold!"

He breathes warm air again. "It gets bigger when it's warm?"

"Hey! Stop that!" I flap him away, but he ignores me and breathes again. "Not warm, it gets bigger when I'm excited, alright!"

"Excited? About what?" He sniffs. "It's not so small now, what are you excited about?"

"Argh! Okay, it gets a little bigger when it's warmer but it gets a lot bigger and harder when I'm excited about, you know, someone. Don't dragons mate?" They must. The whole arrangement with Medvaja came about because of baby dragons rampaging across their western farmlands. I sidle towards my clothes. Strange, they are farther up the beach than I recall, and there is more wet sand.

"Mate? Of course dragons mate, do you think our young hatch from stone eggs?" He looks at me disparagingly. "But you were aroused by the male who works with metal. You cannot mate with him, surely?"

Why must he keep pace with me as I retreat towards my clothes? And why must he keep sniffing my crotch like an overeager hound?

"Of course I can't mate with Seamus," I snap, losing my temper and shoving his head away. "I fuck men because it feels good."

Damir growls and knocks me to the sand. His tongue snakes up and down my torso and for a breath I think he's going to eat me. Then his tongue slides lower and brushes against my cock.

To my mortification, it twitches in response. He licks me again and I stiffen right up.

"You are excited now?" he asks in a low voice.

"Are you… are you going to eat me?" Thankfully my voice holds no tremor, merely a breathiness that has everything to do with the wonderful warm pressure and wetness he's inflicting on me.

He chuckles. "Only a taste."

Surely this is not happening? My cock stands at full attention and I can't think of anything but how good Damir's tongue feels and how ludicrous this situation is. I groan, eyes rolling back as he sweeps across my balls. *Surely he's getting sand in his mouth?* I'm just grateful it doesn't seem to be an issue. I wish he could take me in his mouth but beyond the size difference is the matter of the sharp teeth, so I wrap my fingers and pump, needing the pressure as he swirls and laps.

"No," he says, pausing. "Take your hand away."

"Huh?" I obey, frustrated.

He chuckles again and gives one last lick. "You will wait." He sits back, breathing in deeply.

What in all the ancestors just happened?

"Get into your outer skins, little human. I should take you back to the Weyr."

Six

Damir deposits me, pack and all, at the entrance to Obsidian clan's weyr without a word. I watch him fly away. Shaking my head, I enter the huge cavern to find my way back to Callistemon's personal weyr.

I'm forced to ask for directions through the tunnels a number of times—a mottled grey dragon accompanies me part of the way, shooting sidelong glances like she can't quite believe I'm real. I'm sniffed at, stared at—some dragons stop and stare as I walk past, but I don't mind. No one is unfriendly, or aggressive, and I understand I'm a novelty.

Descending to Callistemon's cave, the orange dragon peers up from her work bench where she is slicing huge blue mushrooms with her claws and dumping them into a cauldron.

"Ah, Eitel. Glad you made it back. Where did you get to today?" She stops, sniffs deeply, then raises her eye-ridges.

"Uh, may I use the bathing pool?" *Can she smell Damir on me? What else can she tell?*

"Of course." It's hard to judge, but her voice sounds suspiciously like it's holding back laughter. I retreat to bathe.

Clean and now hungry, I return and dig through my pack, finding supplies.

"Axel brought fresh meat." Callistemon indicates a smaller, simmering pot. "I added some herbs, nothing medicinal, just flavor."

"Thank you." I find my wooden bowl and use my knife to dig out several large chunks. I suppose they are small cuts to a dragon. *Did I pack a fork? Jep would whack me over the head if I didn't account for my kit properly. Ah, there is it.* "This is really good!" It would have been good even if I wasn't ravenous. A light garlic taste laces the meat, and something else I don't recognize but reminds me of thyme.

Callistemon chuckles. "I spent part of today determining what might be toxic to humans. Wouldn't want to poison you."

I drop my fork. "Oh. How did you work that out?" *Great, now I'll spend the next twelve hours hunched over the privy.*

"I've cared for many dragons and animals. I had a couple of bear cubs once, and they seem similar in their omnivorous habits." She goes quiet. "They were good pets."

I speak slowly, thinking of Axel. "Am I like a pet to you?"

She focuses on me. "No. My bears were clever and mischievous, but you are a more complex creature. You also speak. I've been listening to my patients today. The gossip about what you humans can do is the talk of the Weyr."

What we can do… "I didn't do anything," I say lightly. "Must have been all the others. I know Seamus was forging chain links."

"Indeed. Apparently Muscario has quite changed his opinions on humans since discovering the possibility of weaving 'flags'." She stumbles over the foreign word. "Sapphire clan are arguing over the best design for their own 'flag' and your weaver is sketching plans for a bigger 'loom'."

"Oh? And the others?"

"I believe Amethyst clan are quite enthralled with your musician, and your warrior friend is showing Ruby clan projectile weapons."

I frown. "No one here seemed that interested when I told them about soldiering."

Callistemon hums. "Don't be disheartened. Obsidians tend to be hunters, not fighters. Perhaps tomorrow you can visit your friend staying with Citrine. She is showing them how to work hides to be stronger and more complex."

Even Callistemon doesn't want me around. "Can't I stay with you? I could help… somehow."

She turns amber eyes on me. "Perhaps. I have patients to see in the morning. Damir will be taking me, and he cannot carry us both."

I want to protest that if I rode on his back he could easily carry Callistemon in his claws, but the black dragon has made it *very* clear that isn't a privilege I'll be receiving any time soon.

I finish my stew and settle in for the night, bunking down under my cloak on the bearskin rug again.

I'm woken in the night by a strange noise. The fire has died down to embers, but it seems to be coming from Callistemon's sleeping nook. It's a soft growling, and grunting, rhythmic but not distressed. Is she having a dream? Do dragons dream? I suppose there is no reason they wouldn't.

Lifting a glowing crystal from the covered clay jar that holds them, I peer into the shadows… the moving shadows.

A shape larger than Callistemon alone shifts as my eyesight adjusts. Darker scales than her orange…

A low hum sounds and I see her neck arch, eyes closed. I blink as I comprehend—a black dragon, Damir, twists his neck to glare back at me but doesn't stop his motion. Callistemon writhes underneath him, her growls now obvious to me as pleasure.

I fumble the crystal, covering it with my hands and returning it to the jar. Lying under my cloak, I cannot help but strain my ears to catch every sigh, every grunt, every draconic moan.

I had no idea they were together—how could I have? *Is it normal to swive with others in the same cave? Or do I not count because I'm* just *a human?*

The pace increases, and I'm mortified to find myself hardening. My cock twitches, remembering Damir's tongue on it today. If I touch myself now will they hear? If I find release will they smell it?

Argh! I bite my lip and try to think of other things. Training maneuvers. Jep yelling at me during sword practice. Crossing swords. Big swords. Big… *Argh!*

Damir growls loudly, echoing Callistemon. They fall silent. *Thank the ancestors!* My cock still aches to be touched, but I sternly ignore it.

When I wake in the morning, both dragons are gone.

~ | ~

Irritated by my inadvertent voyeurism last night, I stomp out of Callistemon's weyr and make my way up through the tunnels, chomping angrily on the last piece of stale bread from my pack. I leave most of my gear—food supplies, armor, weapons—but pack some basics into a satchel. Water skin, cheese, apples, dried meat, bowl and spoon. I don't know where I'll end up today but at least I won't be hungry.

At the main cavern entrance, I take in my surroundings. Dragons in varying shades of grey and black fly over me, coming in or heading out.

"Excuse me!" I call to a smaller dragon with scales the color of a raincloud. "How far is it to Citrine clan?" Despite my annoyance at Callistemon, I'll still take her advice and try to visit Nyree.

The dark grey dragon waddles over and peers at me. "Great sky, you really can talk," he says in a gravelly voice.

I give a tight smile. "Yes, sir, I can. Do you know the way to Citrine clan?"

He coughs, then points a claw north-west. "Not far. It's the next weyr over."

Leaving him peering after me, I tramp up and down grassy slopes in the direction he indicated. It takes me an hour, with several detours around gullies, but by keeping an eye on the skies above me I soon discern the direction that yellow-hued dragons are flying to and from.

I find Nyree out in the open fitting a small, buttercup yellow dragon with a harness that secures a satchel to its back. The dragon takes off once Nyree gives the signal, swoops in a wide circle and does several barrel rolls. It crows with delight as the satchel stays closed and doesn't shift. Nyree grins in satisfaction.

"Very impressive." I greet her.

"Eitel!" Her grin broadens into a friendly smile and she dances up to give me a one-armed hug. "How are things going for you? Why aren't you with your clan?"

"Uhh, they suggested I check in on you, say hello." No need to say the Obsidians are disinterested in me and I'm superfluous.

She gives me a knowing look. "I'm fine. Been describing all the things I can make with leather and working out what they might actually find useful. No need for boots or jerkins." She pokes mine.

"We like the idea of having our claws free when carrying," a large golden dragon joins the conversation. It's Councilor Iqbal. "We see the way you humans have your packs, and it would certainly allow fewer dragons to move more things across distance."

I have to wonder what kind of distance he's talking about, since Kyan flew us all the way from Caelon in a day. Are they planning on going somewhere? Or maybe their arms get tired easily, even if it's not that far.

"Leatherworkers are crucial," I chip in. "Whether it's in the army or not. Armor, waterskins, harness…"

"Armor?" Iqbal interrupts.

I exchange a puzzled look with Nyree. "For humans, yes. I don't imagine you'd need it, since your scales look pretty tough."

"Indeed." The golden dragon says no more, but instead asks if we need feeding. "Kyan was most emphatic that we needed to take good care of you, our guests." He gives a smile, and I find myself warming to his steady presence. "I'll take you both to the river where you shall convene with the others."

"Let me take the harness off first," Nyree points to the smaller dragon who has landed nearby.

Despite my annoyance at Callistemon, I'm glad she left the airsickness tonic for me to take because Iqbal's flying is jerky. He does lower Nyree and me gently, at least, then makes a beeline for Kyan, who is fielding questions from the aggressive blue dragon, Muscario. Eveline is watching, arms crossed, a skeptical expression on her face.

"How goes it?" I ask.

She raises an eyebrow, then nods to Nyree and me. "He's a bossy sort." She indicates Muscario. "But he gets things done.

Getting timber cut so I can build a bigger loom, but of course I'm going to need supplies from back home. At least I didn't sleep in a pen last night."

"So you can weave larger pieces?" I move to the fire pit I built yesterday and start arranging wood. *Maybe Liuda can light it.* I glance around, but the small black dragon isn't here yet.

"So I can teach them to weave! They're quite dexterous." Her tone is impressed. "Muscario ordered a number of his clan to study and learn—I think he's determined to prove that anything we can do, dragons can do better." She drops her voice at that last part.

"I'm getting that impression," I say drily. Nyree snorts.

"Evvy!"

We all look up as Axel swoops in, Hartleigh dangling from his claws. The farmer stumbles as he lands but keeps going. "Are ye well? Did they treat ye better?" His concern is genuine, but Eveline flaps a hand.

"I'm fine, ye great lout." They exchange news, Nyree chipping in, while I build the fire and fill the pot from the river. Hartleigh bemoans Malachite clan's lack of interest in what he has to say about farming, and I'm relieved to know I'm not the only one who is being dismissed by their hosts.

An hour later, when we've all eaten our fill of the huge fish Axel proudly deposited, Kyan speaks to us all.

"Things seem to be going well. My fellow councilors have been telling me what they are learning and most agree there is value in human crafts."

"And those that don't?" Captain al Stauberg crosses her arms. Hartleigh grunts in agreement. I chuckle to myself.

Kyan shrugs. "This is why we have a council, not just a single ruler. Things are discussed, and what is best for the Weyr will be decided."

The captain bristles at that, but Monique lays a calming hand on her. "It is more like a guild," she says softly.

"I mean no criticism of Princess Rhea." Kyan cracks a smile. "I, for one, found it very beneficial to deal with a single person when brokering the Treaty."

"I'll bet you did," the captain mutters, then louder, "I just like decisiveness. Our people are at war."

"And Kamelya and Dorukhan are there, assisting your armies with supplies and in any other way they can that does not endanger themselves." Kyan is serious now. "Our people have been isolated pacifists for a long time. I cannot frighten them."

"Pacifists?" Anasta frowns. "Is that why Ruby clan acts so nervous when I describe tactics to them?"

Kyan nods. "Ruby is more aggressive than other clans, but even so it tends to be in shows of strength and agility."

"Huh." I scratch my head. *Explains why Obsidians are so disinterested.*

Captain al Stauberg puts her hands on her hips. "This would have been useful to know *before* we came here!"

"Yatina," Monique murmurs. "Kyan is trying."

"Why?"

Everyone turns to look at me. I cough, but go on. "Why are you trying, Councilor Kyan? Why is this so important to you?" I've had so much idle time lately my brain has been puzzling on this.

The great green dragon bristles. Captain al Stauberg stiffens and suddenly we all remember that this one huge creature could lash out and kill us all at a stroke. Seamus glares at me; Eveline looks terrified.

"I mean no disrespect," I add hurriedly. "I mean, it seems like you all get on very well without human craft. Sure, there are things that could benefit, just like we could with the glowing crystals, but it seems like we need you more than you need us, especially for the war."

A dragon with a pursed expression is a sight I never thought I'd see, but here I am. At least, I *hope* the tension around Kyan's mouth is the equivalent of pursed lips and not preparation to blast me into fiery oblivion.

"Is it not enough that it benefits both our people?" he asks. "We have no nefarious reasons for wanting this alliance."

Captain al Stauberg starts to argue, but Monique touches her shoulder again. The rest of us exchange unsettled looks.

"Another week, and we shall return you to your land and our council will debate what contact with humans should look like. I need them to see we are not so different." Is there a hint of desperation in his voice?

Captain al Stauberg nods, tight-lipped. "I swore to my princess that I would see this endeavor to success. She trusts you, and I also believe you mean us no harm." She glances at Monique. "We are, as you say, not so different."

Something is going on here, some undercurrent of conversation that I cannot read. I often feel this with people, and it often lands me in trouble because I miss the cues that others seem to get, but for once I'm not the only one. Seamus, Nyree—everyone bar Monique seems to be as confused as me.

Our meeting ends and various dragons come to collect their designated human guests. As with yesterday, I'm the last one left, Kyan having taken off early, Axel and Liuda nowhere in sight. Somehow I'm not surprised when Damir alights only after everyone else is gone.

I eye him, my arms crossed. He grins.

"Are you here to take me back to Callistemon?" I enquire, a tremor of anticipation—whether excited or apprehensive, I can't tell—running through me. Why didn't he arrive when the others were still here? Why is he running—flying—around after me anyway? Are the rest of Obsidian Clan truly so disinterested in me?

"She's worn out after her patient visits this morning. She needs rest this afternoon and asked me to... supervise you." He prowls closer and I tense.

"Maybe she was a little worn out from last night?" I challenge. *You are not going to intimidate me, you oversized bat-winged lizard.*

His grin broadens and he leans down, speaking softly. "Did you enjoy watching, little human. Listening to us?"

If he were a man I would shove him. But I can't shove a dragon the size of a small cottage. At least, I shouldn't. Yet somehow my hands find his muzzle and I push firmly. It's so unexpected he rears back.

"You're the one putting on the show, you pervert," I hiss. "And what was yesterday about, on the island? You think I'm some kind of toy?"

His eyes narrow and I'm in the air, ground rushing away before I can blink. "You can't keep doing this!" I yell, hammering at the claws wrapped securely around me. "Ask before you pick me up!"

His only answer is a chuckle as we soar towards the mountains.

Seven

"What is wrong with you?" I demand.

We're east of the Weyr, that much I know, in a high grassy valley bisected by a rushing stream. The icy rivulet cascades off a cliff to join the main river far below. No human could climb here. Once again, I'm at the mercy of a dragon who seems to delight in tormenting me with his company.

Damir cocks his head. "That's a cruel question."

I hesitate, moderating my tone. "What I mean is, why do you keep snatching me up like this? And why is nobody else from Obsidian clan interested in looking after me?"

He shrugs. "Our clans are our families, but we all come and go as we please. Some of us choose to come and go more than others."

"That doesn't answer my question."

The black dragon lowers himself to his belly a little ways from me, watching me. "I told you, Callistemon asked me to keep an eye on you. Most Axinites are dull-headed, but not her."

I put my hands on my hips. "Is that why she lives with Obsidian Clan? She doesn't get along with Axinites?"

He glances away. "They don't appreciate her."

I'm sure there is more to it than that, but I let it go for now. "And why are you interested in talking to me? Kyan said you're all pacifists—is my being a soldier so abhorrent to you?"

He swings his head back in surprise. Bird calls echo through the pine trees that climb the valley walls. It's much cooler here than down in the Weyr, though it has not rained since we left Medvaja. I wait for his answer.

"I've been asked to… get to know you better. Other clans might be swayed by fancy crafts and tricks but Grevillus insisted I find out what humans are like as… as people."

"Huh." I rub my chin. I need a shave. "So he sees us as people? Not animals? Not even pets?"

Damir considers me. "He accepts that you are not animals. But whether you are a threat is another matter. Hence why the others in Obsidian have been ordered to steer clear."

I throw my hands up. "Have you seen us? You're huge, you can fly—some of you can breathe *fire,* for ancestors' sake—how on earth can we be a threat compared to that? Because we have weapons? You *are* weapons. Why do you think the Medvajans want your assistance with the war? Even the sight of one of you will send the Trevi running scared."

Damir cocks his head. "Yet you are not frightened of me?"

I shrug. "You haven't hurt me. Molested me, perhaps."

"Molested?"

I redden. "You know, when you… on the beach…"

He creeps closer. "You seemed to quite enjoy it."

I cross my arms. "You still should have asked."

He leans in and sniffs. "You show me your male appendage, several times, when all the other humans remain covered. Then when I tasted it you became aroused."

"That doesn't mean…" I break off in a cough. Truth be told, the idea of him licking my cock again is quite exciting. I know now Seamus isn't interested, and Hartleigh's not my type, nor I his by the way he fawns over Eveline. But more importantly, I realize I've looked up at dragons flying overhead for several days now, and I've not seen genitalia once. "How do dragons know someone is interested?" I ask slowly.

He blinks. "By scent and display, of course."

"Ah." I slowly take off my jerkin, then my shirt, maintaining eye contact as best I can. His eyes are luminous, the pupils like a cat's. They contract and expand as he takes me in.

"So by displaying myself," I gesture to my crotch, which is already swelling against my breeches, "I'm telling you I'm interested."

"That you wish to copulate, yes." His tongue darts in and out.

"Bit of a size difference, wouldn't you say?" I tuck my thumbs into my waistband and tug down provocatively.

Damir grins. Those teeth should be frightening but I'm too horny to care. "I asked Kyan for a way that I could use the shrinking spell. I'm no mage, but he charmed a tear for me."

This piques my curiosity at the same time as dampening my excitement. "You talked to Kyan about this?" I flick my gaze about the valley, half-expecting the dark green dragon to be hiding behind a rock. The idea of being watched strikes another thought.

"Is that why you went for it with Callistemon last time while I was right there? You like being watched?"

Damir sits back. "Being watched?" He lifts his chin, considering. "It would depend. Some dragons are very private and jealous of their partners. Callistemon and I are not, but she would not display to just anyone. She felt comfortable with you there because she knew you and I had begun to court."

"Court?"

"What would you call it?"

I cough again. "I suppose court is as good a word as any. Does anyone else know? Or just Callistemon and Kyan?" I don't know why I'm embarrassed. Back home I tend to flaunt my sexual escapades, at least to the others in my squad. Some are envious, some just like to live vicariously through me. They know me, however. Damir might say that other dragons see humans as people, but... people are strange when it comes to sex.

Damir shakes his head. "Grevillus may suspect. I reported to him after you bared yourself to me by Callistemon's pool and he instructed me to..."

"Instructed you to what...?" I enunciate my words.

He flicks his eyes down. "As I said before, I find out what humans are like as people."

I digest this information. "So are you doing this because you've been told to?" I'm opportunistic, but even I don't want a pity-fuck.

Damir whuffs warm breath over me. "Is it wrong to admit I'm curious? I smelt Kamelya after those two human females stayed in her weyr, and it got me wondering."

I gape at him. "Which one is Kamelya again?" I scour my brain—Eveline, Nyree, Anasta, Shrusti. Our party was heavily weighted towards women. Then of course there was Monique and Captain… *Oh!*

"She's a red female, a mage. She went with Dorukhan to carry supplies for your human princess." He creeps a little closer.

My mind races even as my pulse quickens. I reach out a hand and tentatively brush his snout. He inhales but doesn't blink.

"So you're just curious, is that it?" His scales are softer than I expected.

"Aren't you?" His voice is a caress that ripples into my soul. I shiver and his nostrils flare. *Right. They smell arousal.*

"So what feels good for a dragon?" I move so I can stroke his cheek, then reach for his neck.

"Harder," he whispers. "I can barely feel you."

I drag my nails along his skin. "I don't have claws. And like I said, there's a bit of a size difference." Thus far my actions are no different to patting a dog or a horse, but unlike an animal, every movement is loaded with a far more intimate feeling. Damir's scent is also far more appealing.

He laughs. "I told you, Kyan charmed a tear for me."

My hand hovers. He twists to look at me and my confusion is evident. He laughs again and reaches for a small woven basket (small for him, it's the size of my head) that he'd dropped to the side when we'd first landed here.

From within the basket, he extracts a luminous green stone about the size of a fist. At least, it looks like a stone, but when Damir hands it to me I exclaim and almost drop it. It's not hard like a stone—it has a rubbery quality—but it's heavy.

"What in all the ancestors…?"

"It's an enchanted tear. I told you I got Kyan to charm one for me." He looks at me expectantly.

"That doesn't tell me what it does…" I heft the tear.

"You eat it."

I glare. "Don't patronize me."

He huffs and butts my chest with his head. I sprawl backwards, clutching the tear but increasingly infuriated. I'm horny and frustrated and now he's trying to make me look stupid. *As if I need help.* "Stop pushing me around!"

He laughs. "Just eat it."

"What will it do?" I demand.

He smirks, darting his tongue out to lick my cheek. "Eat it and find out."

I inhale sharply through my nose. "You're a right tease, you know that?"

He watches with sharp eyes as I lift the tear to my mouth, tentatively nibbling. It reminds me of a summer peach. My teeth puncture the firm skin, releasing a fruity, lush aroma. I inhale, taking it in.

"Go on," he murmurs.

I take a bigger bite. The so-called tear is easy to chew, with a tartness that makes it refreshing. Damir's intense staring makes it a challenge to swallow—is he thinking about what else might go in my mouth? How would that even work? What does a dragon cock even look like?

A strange feeling swells in me. It's not just me getting hard. I'm… bigger. Literally getting bigger. Or Damir is shrinking. *No, I'm definitely growing!*

My boots and breeches are too tight and I yank them off, dropping the remaining half of the teardrop. It bounces away but Damir snatches it up and pops it back into its basket. I only notice because everything is getting further away. The dragon is the same height as me now.

My growth slows. His head is at my chest now, though of course his overall length is greater than my height alone, and if he threw up his wings he would gain the advantage.

"Look at you," he drawls, a predatory smile crossing his face. "Not so little and helpless now."

Huh. I feel powerful. I look at my hands, bigger than his forepaws, and cup his jaw, then slide my fingers down to grasp his neck.

He reacts like a whip crack, pouncing upon me in reaction to the threat. We tumble backwards. The scuffle results in the dragon pinning me to the soft grass, grinding his nether regions against mine. A firm, sinuous length presses against my stomach and groin. I gasp.

"Did you think just because you're larger I would let you dominate me?" He snaps, tension imbued in every part of him.

I wrestle one arm free and reach down to grab the insistent, explorative appendage that seems to have a life of its own. He stills. I stroke down and then up. Damir lets out a low rumble and his anger seems to dissipate.

My own cock is aching, and I press it against his and stroke them both, my grip stretched. As he rears into the pleasure of it I push him back and shift to kneel, releasing my cock but still gripping his.

His strangled sound of surprise makes me grin as I lower my mouth over his pulsating tip. Dragons might have long tongues, but they don't have soft lips like humans and I suction with mine, laving my tongue up and down and pumping his writhing cock with my fist.

The firmness is the same as my own, but his is longer and far more mobile. I can't take the whole length in my mouth, but I try, stopping only when his twitching tip prompts me to cough and gag a moment.

"Are you alright?" He's out and down at my level in a second, forepaws gripping my shoulders.

I cough again and laugh. "Fine. Sorry—wasn't expecting that." Clearing my throat, "Let me go again."

He assesses me, then nods after brief consideration. I grin reassuringly, reaching for his cock again.

"Did it feel good?" I whisper.

Damir nods and growls as I squeeze. I grin again and kiss near the base. He shudders. I kiss my way up and lick the tip, closing my lips around his quivering heat.

"So good," he grunts, thrusting in tiny jerks as the feeling overcomes him. I'm more prepared now, cycling breath through my nose as I take him in, suppressing my gag reflex as he moans.

I withdraw, raking my teeth ever so lightly. Flames seem to light his eyes.

"I'm going to fuck you so hard, little human," he breathes, seeming to forget we are roughly the same size now.

"Oh?" I suck harder, then take a quick breath. "Going to mount me, hold me down?" The thought of being pinned down again, this time with my ass in the air, has me panting.

"Is that what you'd like?" he growls.

I pull back, then slowly turn around, keeping my head turned to watch his reaction as I bare myself to him. I lick my fingertips and trail the moisture between my cheeks. The sensitive skin twitches, even as my balls hang heavy and my cock throbs.

Damir lowers himself and flicks his tongue out, following my lead. I groan. This encourages him to lick more, tormenting my ass with thrilling sensations. I gasp and spread my knees further, grateful for the softness of the grass.

Then he's upon me, claws pricking into my shoulders, wings spread wide above us. His twitching cocktip, still moist from my own mouth, seeks my entrance. *Nudge, nudge.* Despite my magical increase in size, his cock is still large relative to my body, and I feel a bolt of panic that this creature, this dragon, could rend me in two. What if the spell wears off suddenly? I quell my fear and breathe, grateful that the first man who ever fucked me in the ass was experienced and slow, and taught me how to relax into each inch. Any discomfort from the stretch is quickly overtaken by rising, pleasurable fullness. I brace with one hand and fist my cock, letting the gratification melt into every part of me.

Then he twitches, and I can't stop the shout that escapes me as an intense sensation rises through me. Damir twitches again, sinking deeper. He places his jaws lightly on my neck and I'm paralyzed by fear and ecstasy. My cock is already leaking but I can't hold it. It's taking everything I have to brace my hands against the grass and receive each powerful stroke.

Damir is breathing hard. I can't think past, *yes, full, so good, yes* as he hits that magical spot inside me again and again and the feeling builds up and up and I'm yelling again as I burst forth in release, spurting onto the grass. His answering roar echoes through the valley. Several more thrusts and I'm groaning in stupefied joy as he comes inside me. My shoulders burn where his claws have cut in, but I push the pain away, slumping onto my stomach and letting his weight rest on me. His wings curl over, whilst his tail circles my ankle.

"That was good," I half-laugh after a while, our breathing slowing. His heart still thumps against my back, and I revel in the compression his body provides. Safe. Warm. I also feel deliciously used and wanton, but at least he hasn't leapt off straight away.

Damir nips my neck.

"Ow!"

"Mm," he grunts, then settles again. "I like you this size."

"Didn't like me before?" I ask sardonically.

He nips again.

"Ow!"

"Be quiet, Eitel." But his voice has no malice. I close my eyes and smile, wonderfully spent.

Eight

I wake, on my side, curled into the dragon's embrace. His wing blankets my naked form, and I feel… looked after. Dimly, I see that I have returned to my usual size—Damir's bulk is huge at my back. He is still, his breathing deep and regular.

I'm loathe to let go of the sense of peace that pervades me, though I can see the shadows grow long and the cool breeze tickles its way into my warm cocoon. We will have to return to the Weyr soon, and, like every other lover before, Damir will grow distant. Urges and curiosity satiated, he'll move on.

He stirs. I shiver as the cold mountain air darts past his wing, but use that as my prompt to wriggle from his embrace and locate my clothes. My breeches survived, barely. A huge rent in the fabric leaves my right thigh exposed, but I tuck my shirt lower there and fortunately my boots cover the shredded cuffs around my ankles. My jerkin isn't enough to stave off the cold and it is with chattering teeth I turn back to Damir.

"Should we return?"

He regards me inscrutably. "Humans. No wonder you need extra skins."

Annoyed, I shoot back. "I know! Are you going to let me freeze or are you going to take me back to the Weyr?"

His eye ridges shoot up. "I thought you wished me to ask if I may pick you up?" he says solicitously.

I start to speak, then glare. "Don't suppose you'll let me ride?"

He smirks. "Next time, perhaps."

Heat rushes through me as I catch his meaning. Stupidly pleased, I run my hand through my hair and cough. "Pick me up then."

We're up and away and I'm grateful for the small windbreak his claws provide, something that wouldn't be present on his back. *Perhaps I can borrow a fur from Callistemon's cave.*

My teeth are chattering by the time we land and I stumble through tunnels, Damir in the lead, to Callistemon's homely cavern. I'm hungry but I need to defrost first.

"May I use the pool?" I ask. At least we're out of the wind.

"Of course?" She looks over Damir and me and sniffs, then gives a small smile. I flush. "Perhaps we will join you."

Ancestors. Is she going to expect sexual favors now?

My tension must be obvious as I cling to one side of the warm pool, waiting for the surface to settle as the two dragons slide in. There is not much room left, but they appear content to soak in stillness.

"Do not fear advances from me, Eitel," the orange dragon pronounces, clearly amused. "I am not seeking copulation, just a bath."

"Ah." I clear my throat. "I should clarify, for my sake, and other humans, that we can't hide away our... private parts. If we are naked it doesn't always mean we are seeking... sex."

"I did wonder," Damir answers casually. "But you became aroused anyway when I licked you there, so I continued."

"Alright!" *Ancestors, just tell everyone!* "Is that why you changed your tune about me so quickly? Because you thought I was... showing interest?"

Damir looks away.

Callistemon laughs. "I think it made him realize that you aren't just an animal."

He huffs in embarrassment. "I'm not a degenerate who goes around violating non-sentient beasts."

Callistemon laughs again. "I for one am pleased for you both that you are copulating. Damir seems less anxious about the so-called 'threat' humans pose to our way of life. He's so uptight."

Damir growls without rancor.

I scratch my head. "You do not mind it?" I ask her. I sense not, but it's always nice to confirm.

She shakes her head, causing ripples in the water. "Damir seeks other partners from time to time. I do not, for most others find me… unnatural."

"They are bigoted fools." This time his growl is real.

A wave of sadness washes over me as surely as the lapping pool. "Because of your wings," I say.

The silence speaks for itself.

I soak in the warm water, then blurt out, "My older sister is deaf. I often heard the neighbors say how she'd never get married, since no one would want a wife who couldn't hear her baby cry. Sometimes men in the village would joke that they'd marry her, since they'd never have to listen to her nag." I pause, remembering. "I used to get into fights over that. My cousin Jep usually had to step in because I'd get thrashed. It was so unfair though! My sister is the kindest, most loving soul. None of them were good enough for her, anyway." I trail off.

The dragons listen. I feel they understand.

"Are you that poor of a fighter?" Damir ventures.

"Damir!" Callistemon nips him.

"What?" he retorts. "He is larger than every other human in his group, except the male who does not wish to copulate with him. And he is a soldier. Why did his cousin have to rescue him?"

I snap from my funk and give a half-hearted chuckle. "I was thirteen. Didn't get this tall until I hit my twenties. And I tended to just charge in without thinking, didn't matter how many of them there were."

"Ah." Damir subsides a moment. "You did say you were too stupid to be afraid."

"Damir!" Callistemon swings her head and smacks him in the neck this time. The wave that results submerges me and I lose my grip on the edge laughing.

"It's fine!" I choke back my guffaws. "*I* said it, not him!"

She shakes her head and clambers out. "He's so rude. I'm sorry, Eitel."

Damir is unapologetic. "She is too kind to people. I balance her out."

"I balance you out!" she calls back as she exits the bathing cave.

I smile, not missing the affectionate look the black dragon shoots after his... mate? Partner? I suppose this is the opportunity to ask and find out.

~ | ~

Morning sees Callistemon out on her rounds again.

"I'll come and find you later," Damir promises, and returns my bashful smile with a ferocious grin of his own. "Shall we visit the island again?"

"You've got him in heat, Eitel." Callistemon smirks.

"Quiet, you, or I'll drop you in the river." The care with which he gathers her in his claws belies his words, and soon he is winging away from the entrance of the Weyr, a smaller orange shape carried by a larger black one.

I hike over to see Nyree. I'm not halfway there when a shadow sweeps over me and Axel circles in to land.

"Hello!" His very being exudes cheerfulness, and despite his initial comments about keeping humans as pets, I like the enthusiastic green dragon.

"Good morning, Axel," I call, waving.

He barrels to a stop a little too close for comfort, but doesn't flatten me, so I consider that a win.

"What are you doing out here by yourself? I was heading into the mountains to hunt—you humans sure eat constantly—when I saw you. Aren't you meant to be with Obsidian? Does Kyan know?"

"It's alright!" I assure him. "Damir had to take Callistemon out so I thought I'd walk over to Citrine. I know the way."

He hops closer. "Would you like me to take you? You can ride on my back if you like... oh. Oh!" He crouches low and sniffs me.

"What?" I'm alarmed.

Axel clears his throat. "You, uh, oh my. Um, never mind, I don't want to clip wings, it was just a friendly offer, nothing more." He beats his wings, almost flattening me with the gale, and takes off. I'm left bemused.

My suspicions increase as I reach Citrine's Weyr and any dragon that lumbers near to investigate veers off the moment they get downwind of me.

Nyree acts no differently, however. She is pleased to have some assistance with tying leather straps and plaiting different colors into ornamental braids.

"They're a lot quieter today," she comments as we sit in the shade of an overhang. "Yesterday I had no shortage of volunteers. I hope the novelty hasn't worn off."

"Yeah, me too," I say with sinking feeling.

When Iqbal appears to take us to our midday meeting with the others, he sports all the formality of his council role, but I swear he is more reserved than yesterday. He carries us to the meeting place by the river, then I catch him sniffing his claws as he waits for Kyan quite a few dozen yards upstream.

"Ho there!" Hartleigh calls, looking relieved. "I've made progress with my clan."

As Eveline, Shrusti, Seamus and Monique join us, he tells everyone how he sparked Malachite clan's interest by asking about seasons and phases of the moon. While they don't farm, they follow celestial events closely for the purposes of hunting and fishing and keep a detailed calendar. I realize that rather than being a simple farmer, Hartleigh is quite a knowledgeable land manager—something my parents probably wish I was. Eveline falls into a discussion with Shrusti about music—turns out she loves to sing—and once Anasta and Captain al Stauberg arrive with Kyan, Seamus is drawn into a discussion about armor and weaponry. I concentrate on gutting the fish we've been supplied and building the fire pit. Nyree helps, and when the food is ready I sit off to the side.

The artist, Monique, sits next to me. "It's certainly been an experience," she observes, nibbling her skewered fish delicately. She doesn't have a Medvajan accent, but certainly isn't from

Huon. South, perhaps? Uraidla or the Empire?

"What brought you into all this?" I eye her skeptically.

She smiles, a truly lovely sight. If I was interested in women I'd string my bow for her in a heartbeat, but by the way she looks at Captain al Stauberg, I'd say she fancies men as much as I fancy women.

She flicks her braid over one shoulder. "Yatina had me come draw the dragons on an Exchange, so people in Zivalj could see what they looked like. That's where I met Kamelya and Dorukhan. I ended up painting for Kamelya as well."

I mull over my next words. "You and Kamelya… and Captain al Stauberg…" I trail off, letting her make of it what she would.

She turns a polite but inscrutable expression onto me. "We have become good friends."

"Hmm." I nod. "I think Damir of Obsidian Clan and I are becoming… good friends."

Surprise and amusement light her face. "Oh, yes?"

I grunt in the affirmative.

"How are you finding… this friendship?"

I give her a sidelong glance but can't stop the small lift at the corner of my lips. "It's… interesting." My half smile falls away. "But I don't know if the other dragons sense it. They are acting strange."

She looks over at Kyan, Iqbal, the blue dragon whose name I can't remember and several others. Their discussion is quiet but appears agitated. The blue dragon is shaking his head vehemently.

Monique looks troubled. "I don't know. Certainly I have not discussed it with any of the dragons in Quartz. It's none of their business. But they have all been polite to me."

"No one has been rude," I protest. "Just strange."

The cause of their strangeness heaves into view. Damir has finished transport duties early and wings his way to join us.

"Are you ready to go, Eitel?" He asks, claws twitching as though he'll snatch me up with or without my consent.

"A word, Damir," Iqbal calls from the conference of his

fellows. The violet dragon is shaking with suppressed laughter. Damir's posture becomes immediately defensive, his expression mulish as he slouches over to the other dragons, tail whipping defiance.

"Oh, boy," I mutter.

"Let's get closer and listen," Monique throws her empty skewer in the fire and wipes her hands on her long tunic. Captain al Stauberg shoots a wary glance, but Monique subtly waves her off.

Under the guise of washing our hands in the river, we drift closer, engaged in inane talk, trying to pick up the threads of the draconic conversation.

"You should not have done it, Damir," Iqbal admonishes.

"Can a human even agree to such a thing?" It's the blue dragon.

"It's listening…" the violet dragon has quicker eyes than the rest, and our eavesdropping is cut short.

Monique bows elegantly, so I salute. "I'm sorry," she smiles disarmingly. "Is there a problem?"

"No," Damir shoots back. Kyan quells him with a look.

"Is this something I want discussed in front of everyone?" I venture, heart sinking.

"Given what I know of humans, no," Kyan intones. "Damir, you may take your human and go. Please explain to him what you have done."

Baffled, I raise eyebrows to Monique.

"Good luck," she whispers.

I collect my satchel and grunt a farewell to the others. "What's got him in a mood?" I hear Eveline say.

"A chafed palm," Seamus replies disparagingly.

Incensed, I stomp over to where Damir waits, wings already half-extended. "Let's go."

I don't appreciate the view as we soar over the coastline, ruminating instead on everyone's callous opinions. *Must I be cheerful all the time?* I think blackly. *Seamus is a dour bastard but the moment I show a little grimness everyone reels in horror.*

"Why do you smell so angry?" Damir calls over the wind.

I want to bristle, but that would involve flexing, which might involve him losing his grip, which would entail me plunging to my death in the ocean below, so I refrain.

"Just tell me what's going on when we land!" I yell back.

We land, on the same little island as before. A favorite spot of his? The sand is still grey, the beach smaller than I remember, but it is peaceful, much like the high valley he took me to. *Do all dragons seek out such solitary places?*

"Right." I've got the trick of getting my balance upon hitting the ground, and my hands are on my hips before Damir has even touched the sand. "What was all that about?" He's carrying the little basket again, the one with the enchanted tear. "Actually, give me that." I point and he offers it up without question. I'm so used to trying to get people to like me I need any advantage I can get. I put the basket at my feet, within easy reach. "Tell me what's going on?"

The black dragon looks away. "Some of the others are angry because I scent-marked you."

"You what?" Nonplussed, I cross my arms over my chest.

He glances sideways at me. "I scent-marked you. I marked you as mine, and they are arguing over whether I should be allowed to do it. Like it is any of their business," he adds in a mutter."

"It's my business!" I retort. "You could have told me!"

His head snaps around. "You enjoyed our time together. You want more, don't you? I want more."

His intensity triggers me into action. I lift the tear from the basket, take a bit and shrug out of my shirt as quickly as I can. Another bite and my boots and breeches are off. A third bite and I decide that will make my point, so I put the remaining portion back in the basket even as I feel my body swell.

I kneel, one palm on the ground to keep my balance as I magically grow. Shaking off the dizziness, I look eye to eye with the dragon who wants to fuck me.

"I do want more," I growl. "But what in all the ancestors is scent-marking? You think I belong to you now?"

His wings flare—he's not backing down. "It's not forever,"

he snaps. "But I didn't want anyone else getting their claws into you. Fearful dullards, they just see you as clever ways of making tools. They'll use you."

"Didn't you use me?" I grab his throat, not hard, but to bring my face close.

"You wanted it," he snarls.

With my increased size comes enough strength to flip him onto his back. His wings flare in an effort to slow his fall and the sand cushions his landing. I straddle him, pinning his wings and stop. I can feel how delicate the bones are, see how thin the wing membrane is.

Without a word, I trail my hands down his chest. His cock is out and erect, so I let my fingertips brush it. His lip curls back in a snarl for a moment, then he returns to watching me.

Slowly, I grip his cock. Unlike a human appendage, soft, thin scales spiral up from base to tapered tip. They are lighter in color than the rest of him, but only just, a beautiful dark grey that looks like washed stone. It's warmer than a human cock too, something I noticed when he was in me the day before. I shiver at the thought of him filling me again, and part of me is tempted to sit on that glorious heat, but I have a need to take him too. To show him that I will not be simply possessed and fucked, but I will possess him. Too many lovers have simply enjoyed me then moved on, and I have let them.

Stroking slowly, I watch Damir's eyes flutter close. I slide down, seeking the entrance that lies near the base of his tail. His breath hitches I test the scales that get softer and hotter. I suck my fingers then let them drag gently across his hole. He growls and pushes against my touch, inviting me in.

I slick saliva on my own cock and match the rhythm I'm using on his, then nudge my hardness against him, slipping my way in.

His growl is unearthly as I rock my way into him, fraction by fraction. Damir claws at the ground and pants, pushing against me, trying to take me in faster. I grip his cock and still.

"You'll take me when I say so," I whisper. "Don't rush me, dragon."

Honestly, the slow pace is as much for my sake as for him, because if I fuck him any faster I'll blow like a youth in a whorehouse, and I want to make this last. This is not a quick swive, to be forgotten. I want him to know I'm in control.

For now. The deeper I get the harder it is to fight the urge to just pound away. Damir's rumbles of pleasure vibrate through my cock and when his tail curls at my throat I almost lose my mind.

"You want me to go harder?" I growl. His tail tightens aggressively, not choking me but threatening.

"Can you?" he smirks. "Humans are so soft."

I slam into him and he bucks, his wings curling. Again, and Damir arches. His tail lashes, then returns to my neck. The inherent danger in it all, that I'm fucking a creature who could tear me to shreds with tooth and claw, sends me into a pounding frenzy. I grasp his cock and jerk him frenetically, relishing how he writhes against my hand.

My vision narrows, and I feel more than see the splash of his release all up my chest. The heat surrounding my cock is exquisite, and I slam and slam, feeling my balls tighten. My own heat concentrates and builds up until there's nothing left to do except explode into him with a shout.

Riding that high for a moment, a laugh escapes me. My cock spasms the last few spurts and I shudder, dizzy with euphoria and lack of blood in my brain.

Then I collapse. I'm just sensible enough to avoid putting pressure on his wings, but my head hits his chest with an "oof" from the dragon.

"Sorry," I mutter, breathless.

Damir's growl subsides into a purr and his arms close around me. His heart beats a solid bass to my faster tempo, but my breathing slows as I soak in the sun on my back and his heat from below.

"Scent-bonding makes this all more intense," he murmurs. "I thought you would enjoy it more. I wanted you to enjoy it more."

Drowsily, I remember the source of our argument. "You still should have told me," I sigh. "I would have said yes."

Nine

This time I am awake when I shrink to my normal size. That doesn't stop Damir teasing me with licks until I'm scrabbling for another bite of the enchanted tear so he can fuck me again properly. His tongue is amazing but his cock does wonders for my mood. With him on his back again I ride him until he insists on taking me on all fours again.

"Just need to be in charge, don't you?" I grunt in time with each delicious thrust. The sand under my knees and palms provides soft yet compact resistance so I can brace as he plunges into me.

He slows to a teasing pace. I growl. He chuckles darkly. "No one has ever taken me on my back before. I like these different positions you humans have, but sometimes…" he slams in and my eyes roll back in my head. "Sometimes… traditional ways have their advantage."

He slams in again. I moan.

"For instance…" *Slam.* "I can balance above you using my wings…" *Slam.* "And rake my claws down your back." He slows again and I whimper, *whimper*, for ancestors' sake! The tracing of his claws on my skin sends me into paroxysms of ecstasy.

It's so unlike anything I've had with other men. Some are rough, some are gentle. Damir's firm but sensual touch keeps bringing me to the edge then pulling me back. If this is the result of scent-bonding, then sign me up for another round. It's the best sex I've ever had.

~|~

"Why did you scent-mark me?" I ask again later. The sun sinks into the western sea and I know we'll have to fly back soon.

Damir lifts his head from where he's been dozing on the cooling sand. I loll against his belly, dressed after bathing in the sea with him.

"I told you, I wanted you to enjoy it more." His rumble holds a hint of hurt.

"I know, and I do!" I hasten to reassure him. "I guess I'm not used to lovers worrying so much about what I like." *Ugh, that makes me sound pathetic.* "I mean," I shrug helplessly, staring down the beach, "usually I just wanted to fuck so if they were interested I let them take the lead."

He is quiet for a while. "Should I ask you what you like more?" An awkward silence. "You have said a number of time I need to ask you before I do things, and I have not." He sounds embarrassed.

I pat his flank. "I think what you explained to me last night about dragons knowing so much by scent is why. I mean, plenty of humans don't ask, they just do, and we can't smell each other's emotions. We rely on words and appearances, but they can be faked."

"I will try to ask more," he avows. "Perhaps there is a spell or charm that will give you dragon powers of scent. I will ask Kyan. Then you will know whom to trust."

"Do you want to turn me into a dragon?" I joke, but his words have me thinking. *Then you will know whom to trust.* He needs to know who is safe, and who is a threat.

He is quiet. "Would that be such a bad thing? I know it is not possible, but do you not enjoy it here? Away from your wars— we can swim and fly and be with each other."

His words move me. *He actually wants me to stick around?* No man has ever wanted more than just a fun time with me.

He continues, warming to his theme. "You could live with us in Callistemon's weyr. She enjoys talking to you. You see her as a person, not a crippled dragon. She can tell these things."

My heart bruises that the first person to ever want me, really want me, is not even human. That we might form our own little clan, a cheerful band of misfits. I could learn draconic medicine, help her with her rounds, because ancestors' know I need some activity, some purpose. It would be nice to heal, not just fight.

But there is no question about what is the right thing to do.

"I have a duty to return," I tell him sadly. "My cousin, my comrades, my prince. I'm a soldier of Huon. I cannot abandon my people—that would be treason, and it would be cowardly."

Damir twists his neck to bring his snout close to my body and inhales deeply. "I understand, even though I can smell your sadness."

I half-laugh. "You're like a giant hound, snuffling me constantly." I pat his head and look him in the eyes. No hound ever gazed so acutely, sharp intelligence topping a warm, beating heart. "Unfortunately, it's not a choice. I must."

"It could be a choice," he insists. "Can your prince cross the mountains and fetch you home? I think not."

"What if your council were to insist?" I prod. "There are politics and treaties and bigger things than you or I at stake."

He grumbles. I laugh.

"You really don't like being told what to do!" I tease.

"You like being told what to do a little too much!"

My laughter dies. He's right, in a way. I've always let others take the lead, in sex, in life. No wonder I ended up in the army. I take a deep breath.

"It's still the right thing to do. After the war I would like to come back though. If you want me to."

He inhales deeply again, then rests his head against my chest. I cradle it. Warm, safe, wanted.

~ | ~

We fly back from the island, aiming for Obsidian Weyr but diverting when Axel shoots past us in a hurry.

"Kamelya and Dorukhan are back!" he hollers. "Kyan has called a meeting!"

I'm glad to be in Damir's claws, not on his back as he banks sharply and we spiral down to the council amphitheater.

"Steady on," I yell, but he's already pulling up in a skilled swoop, letting me down gently then soaring away again.

"I will bring Callistemon!" he calls.

Other dragons circle into their tiers, their attention on the huge black dragon, Dorukhan, and the red female, Kamelya, who flop exhaustedly in the center. Kyan speaks rapidly to them, while Captain al Stauberg rubs Kamelya's flank soothingly. I can either hover awkwardly where I am or join them, since I have no inclination to walk over to Seamus and Shrusti, huddled as they are to one side.

"Eat this." I recognize the shimmery, lilac thing that Kyan is offering to Dorukhan as a tear. *I wonder what that one does.* The remnants of the 'grow bigger' tear nestles safely in my satchel.

"Are they alright?" I ask the Captain. She glances at me in surprise.

"Flew hard to get here," she replies shortly.

My stomach sinks. *What happened?* She's not my superior officer exactly, but she's the human authority in this place, so I shouldn't question her, but…

She must read my expression because she snaps, "I don't know any more than you do, soldier. Let them recover and we'll find out!"

Anasta barrels up at a run, having just landed nearby. She catches the captain's words and exchanges a tight look of understanding with me. She wants orders, just like I do.

The amphitheater is almost full when Damir returns, cradling Callistemon to his belly. "Get out of the way!" he snarls as he lowers her carefully to the earth. It's unnecessary—other dragons shuffle surreptitiously away from the orange healer. I frown and meet her as she crosses the center towards the returned dragons.

"I don't know what's happened," I say, placing my hand on her neck. Her pupils are expanded, she seems anxious amidst so many of her kin.

"We'll find out," she grinds out, words muffled by the basket clutched in her teeth.

I fall back, touching Damir as he glares around. "Is she alright?" I murmur.

"She doesn't like crowds," he growls.

I take up a guard position with him as Callistemon consults with Kyan. "I just gave them something for their fatigue," he tells her.

"We bear no injury," Dorukhan rumbles.

"You're full of dung," Kamelya snaps. "He deflected a volley of arrows from me and is lucky to not have a shredded wing! I half carried him here!"

No wonder she looks shattered! She's not a small dragon, like Axel or Liuda, but Dorukhan is huge.

"Let me see the wound," Callistemon insists.

While she fusses, Kyan steps away and takes up a place in the center of the amphitheater. Iqbal, who has been watching closely, swings his tail and strikes the gong for silence. The anxious chatter dies down as dragons wait to hear what he says.

"Thank you for assembling at such short notice." Kyan's voice fills the space. An errant dragon wings its way to the top tier, while the rest lean in to listen. "Our ambassadors to the east have returned with grave news. Our new human allies are under siege from their enemy, trapped between floodwater and an army. We have sought to provide passive aid, bringing supplies, but their enemy attacked Kamelya and Dorukhan too."

Outrage and shock bubble through the councilors and other dragons.

"They are animals," shouts a sky blue dragon. "We should never have gone east."

"Silence!" Iqbal booms, just as Muscario, the leader of the Sapphire clan, turns on the sky blue dragon and snarls.

"Forgive my wingkin," Muscario rumbles. I'm surprised. I remember him being intransigent upon our arrival, and Eveline getting treated like a dog.

Kyan waits a beat then continues. "I ask the council send a full wing to drive back the attackers."

My heart lifts. *Yes!* This is what we came for. The Trevi soldiers would be whimpering in their boots if half a dozen full-grown dragons swooped out of the cloud. It might even win the war.

The next words puncture my buoyancy.

"This is war-mongering!" Grevillus rumbles. "We stand for peace."

"We didn't want this war either!" Captain al Stauberg shouts but she is spoken over by Kyan.

"If we do not defend ourselves and our allies, who is to say these humans will not come for us next?"

"The mountains lie between us," a white dragon drawls.

"Not between our hatchlings, they don't!" Gyeltshen, leader of the Amethyst clan, swings her head in distress. "That is why we sent Kyan in the first place! To protect them!"

"We must not rush into anything." Muscario is adamant. "Let us discuss and debate. Kyan, this includes you. Don't think you can act unilaterally."

"Agreed," Iqbal adds.

Behind me, Dorukhan raises his voice in protest, but not at the prospect of debate.

"You will need to walk out of here and rest that wing!" Callistemon insists. "Otherwise wait until Kyan can enchant you smaller and someone can carry you out."

"This is humiliating," Dorukhan argues.

Callistemon glares. "Just be glad it's not permanent," she hisses, "or you'd be on the ground for the rest of your days."

The large, black dragon seems to realize what he's said, and to whom, and shuts up. Callistemon turns to Damir, who is facing outwards and watching the crowd, but listening in intently.

"I'm done here," she says shortly, sealing a jar of salve and packing it into her basket.

Damir nods, glares at Dorukhan, and opens his wings. He then stops, and hunches down. "Get on," he tells me.

I blink in surprise, and he huffs impatiently. "Unless you want to stand around here while they debate? It took them weeks to agree to send Kyan east the first time."

Weeks? I glance at Captain al Stauberg. Her lips are tight. No human is getting a voice in the shouting match that is going on overhead. We are trapped here until they decide we can or should leave. And all this while our comrades are trapped in a siege by an enemy that is proving far more tenacious that we imagined. Not that it's my job to imagine. I'm just a grunt. I should be back there, following Jep's orders. Not here frolicking on a beach with a dragon. Frustration and shame boils in me.

"Let's go," I mutter, and climb his foreleg to straddle the base of his neck. Damir leaps into the air, beats his wings steadily to hover over Callistemon and gather her up. I feel how much harder he has to work to gain height with her weight as well, but he still has plenty of strength to glare at the dragons who smirk or look away from the ungainly couple. My anger surges in their direction as well.

Obsidian Weyr is almost empty, with every dragon over at the council amphitheater. Damir lets Callistemon down gently, tenderly brushing a claw over his mate's neck as he lets her go. It isn't until he lands nearby and I slide down that I realize it's the first time I've ridden on him rather than being held. *Makes sense, he had to carry Callistemon.* But it warms me, knowing that he was happy to take me with rather than leave me at the council.

"You are tired and stressed from dealing with those ungrateful idiots," he tells Callistemon. "And you are frustrated and angry because you are helpless to assist your people," he says to me. "Let's all get in the hot pool and calm down somewhat."

"I don't want to calm down," I protest. "I want to go back to where I should be, defending my people!" I clench my fists. It's pointless taking out my anger on him but who else is there? Jep would tell me to pull my head in, or we'd throw a few punches until the anger was out.

Damir sniffs me, then looks at Callistemon. She sighs. "I'm sorry our people are so slow to act, Eitel."

"Why? Why are they so… so… passive?" I'm trying not to shout. Good thing there is no one else around. The last thing I need is another dragon getting insulted and telling the council that humans are ill-mannered and demanding as well as violent.

Callistemon shrugs helplessly. "We have lived in isolation too long. None of them wants to risk their wings against your darts or spears." Her lip curls. "They are terrified of becoming a dirt-grubber like me."

"Cowards," snarls Damir.

"Not everyone is as fiercely protective as you, my dear," she says. "You take risks where others fear to."

I shake my head. "We risk losing limbs, yet we still fight."

"You have something to fight for." Callistemon's tone is gentle. "It wasn't until our hatchlings were dying in such numbers that we finally stirred to action."

"Why don't you raise them here, where they are safe?"

Both Damir and Callistemon baulk, and the explanations that follow make me realize dragons are not maternal, that hatchlings are ravenous, feral creatures, and it is only as they reach some sort of maturity and develop innate language they migrate back to the Weyr like homing pigeons.

"Alright, alright," I wave a hand, finding it hard to believe that rational, adult dragons emerge with no parenting. "None of this helps right now." I trudge through the tunnels to Callistemon's cave and flop down on my sleeping nest. The orange dragon disappears through to the bathing pool, but Damir hovers.

"I understand, Eitel." His voice is strained. "Don't think I don't."

I look up at him, confused.

"When you came here, I was very suspicious." He looks away. "Even when I wanted to explore you, I was still wary that you might mean harm to Callistemon, or to the others here."

I nod. I've seen how he is. "She called you protective."

He ducks his head. "Yes. And I pushed you to find out what you were like. I wanted you, but I also wanted to make sure you wouldn't turn on us."

I feel like I'm missing something. "Go on," I say slowly.

"It's why I scent-marked you. It's a way of strengthening a bond."

"Oh." He thought that if we were fucking, and I loved it, I would be less of a danger to him and those he cares about. It's almost naïve in its simplicity, and rather than angering me, I feel for him. Hadn't I slept with so many men in the vague hope they'd care about me?

"Eitel?" he sounds wary.

I focus on Damir. "I think you and I have more in common than you realize." I smile to show him I hold no malice.

"You are not angry?"

"No," I say honestly. "But I still need to go back and protect *my* people too."

He is silent, then nods. "I respect that. I will help where I can."

My heart swells at his offer. Ancestors know I need all the help I can get. *But what can I actually do? I'm just one man.*

"Will *that* help you?"

He's talking about the enchanted tear, still in my satchel. "Perhaps," I say slowly. "It's not as though clothes or armor grow with me, so I'd be pretty vulnerable in a fight." My brain searches for an advantage the tear could give me. Giant me can still be stuck full of arrows. I could give it to Prince Gereon or Princess Rhea—both fierce warriors, but they'd face the same dilemma. It's a pity they can't just challenge the Trevi king to one on one combat. Either of them would wipe the floor with him.

An idea comes to me slowly. Damir sniffs and cocks his head quizzically.

"Can you take me back there?" I ask. "I won't ask you to fight, or put yourself in danger, but... I have a plan."

Ten

The wind whips harshly as we leave the mountains and descend over rain-soaked Medvaja. I'm rethinking the privilege of riding on Damir's back—clinging to his neck ridges for hours at a time requires far more energy than being carried in the safe cage of his claws. On the other hand, probably best he conserves *his* energy for flying, rather than focusing on not dropping me. Puts the onus of staying alive back on me, which is probably for the best.

At least once we're over the lowlands it's easier to stop, rest and scoff some food. Dragons don't need to eat nearly so often, but part of our supplies includes chunks of giant mushroom grown in Callistemon's cave.

"It'll keep him going without slowing him down," she told me as we tied the basket tightly closed for him to carry.

"Your friend with the leather certainly has the right idea with harnesses," Damir grunted. It was the other reason I was riding—we didn't have time to pinch Nyree's harnesses and fit to Damir's form, so he needed his claws free to carry any supplies.

Those claws are currently wrapped gently around me while his wing shelters me from the rain. We've stopped in a sodden field, probably less than an hour's flight from Caelon. I'm pathetically grateful for Damir's warmth, and my great idea of the night before seems naïve and ill-conceived now.

"Are you going to get into trouble from the council?" I ask, trying to not to think about whether I'll be in trouble for going rogue. It's not as though Captain al Stauberg is my commanding officer, but she was the closest thing to it, and I don't like not asking for orders.

Damir snorts. "You worry too much."

Do I? I feel adrift, acting on my own behest. Part of me wants to run straight to Jep when we arrive and ask him to tell me what to do. But he might stop me. Prince Gereon might stop me. I feel the only chance that this will work is if we have the complete element of surprise.

And you want to prove you're not just a useless grunt. There is that too. Something about not having someone telling me what to do all the time has made me see that I can think for myself, at least some of the time.

"Well, then," I roll my stiff shoulders. "Let's get this over with."

~ | ~

"I'm here to parley!" I yell as the Trevi soldiers approach, keeping me firmly at spear point.

"Keep your hands where we can see them!" the sergeant barks. "Remove his weapons."

They strip my sword and knife, pat me down roughly but let me keep holding the square of damp white cloth I'd been flapping frantically as I slowly walked up to the Trevi palisade.

"What do you want?" the sergeant demands.

I look shifty, not exactly difficult considering I'm cold and wet and my large shoulders are hunched in. "I want to speak to your king."

The soldiers all burst out laughing. The sergeant doesn't crack a smile. "King Thetin doesn't talk to the likes of you. Your princess insults us by sending a lout like you. What kind of pathetic surrender is this?"

"It's not surrender." My teeth want to chatter so I grit my jaw. "They don't know I'm here."

The mood immediately darkens. "A traitor?" The sergeant's eyes narrow and his soldiers mutter.

"I'm not Medvajan," I say quickly. "I'm Huonese." Trust

these idiots not to be able to hear the difference in accents. Mind you, I find their northern cadence difficult to follow at times.

"Still a traitor," the sergeant growls.

"I have information for your king about the dragons. On their weaknesses. On their plan to attack." The words come out in a rush. Everyone stills.

This sergeant would give my cousin a run for his money when it comes to implacable expressions. Perhaps it's something they teach sergeants in particular. His eyes search mine and I gulp. I'm a terrible liar.

"Those winged monsters?" Whether I'm lying or not, the sergeant knows he can't risk passing up the opportunity to learn something. Dragons probably exist in myth for the Trevi, much like they do for Huon. Only the Medvajans have had to deal with them in their farthest west, and until recently, thought they were feral beasts the size of a small cottage. No one really considered that they grew much, much larger, and no one here knows that they are risk-averse, pacifists.

"Bind his hands," the sergeant orders. "Bring him."

~ | ~

We cross into camp and I'm pleased to note that defenses are minimal at the rear. The palisade faces the besieged town of Caelon, and clearly the enemy feels a sneak attack is unlikely, as it would require the defenders to slip out via treacherous floodwaters and encircle the Trevi camp. Moving any significant number of soldiers that way would be too dangerous and too noticeable.

Fortunately my plan involves being noticed, though it is no less dangerous.

They march me to a large tent, hands bound behind my back. I've plaited my hair into several sections, binding the last chunk of enchanted dragon tear into one braid than hangs beside my face. It looks like a piece of polished stone or amber. Several bones and feathers hang in other braids, making me look like a wild forest priest with my rough stubble and unkempt clothes. I counted on them taking my weapons, but I hope that disguising the tear will give me the advantage I need for this plan.

The capturing sergeant confers quietly with the guards at the open tent flap, then one of them disappears inside, returning several minutes later. I'm escorted in.

Half a dozen hard-faced men and women stand around a table. It's a battle map. Blue cloth marks the rivers, a carved wooden house signifies Caelon between them. Figurines of men and horses cluster but before I can see them all, a young man with a bright shock of red hair gestures, and someone flicks their cape over the table.

The young, red-haired man looks me up and down. His angular face misses nothing, and I sense despite his youth he is used to making decisions.

My guess is confirmed when the sergeant bows. "Your grace, this prisoner claims to be a Huonese defector with information on the dragons we saw."

The young Trevi king never takes his eyes off me. "Is that so?"

I try not to squirm. I'm a terrible liar so I steel myself to tell part-truths. Bowing, I keep my eyes on his boots.

"Your grace, my name is Eitel Jarvo and I wanted to warn you about the dragons. My own prince has been duped by them and their devious intentions, and that of the Medvajan princess."

At the mention of Princess Rhea, King Thetin's jaw tightens.

"Your prince is married to the Medvajan princess," he states flatly. "They are allies."

"She has tricked him!" I shoulder my plait into my mouth, as if chewing nervously. It doesn't actually matter how spurious my claims sound, I've achieved stage one; get near the king.

Time for stage two.

I rip the enchanted tear from my plait with my teeth, chewing and trying not to gag on the stray hairs that come with it.

"What *is* he doing?" a woman's voice asks, sounding disgusted.

The sergeant grabs my arm and forces me upright, frantically patting me down. "Nothing!" he shouts, then flinches when he feels my bicep bulge.

This is going to hurt. It does, but only for a fraction of second as the bindings burst free from my wrists. Everything else bursts free as my clothes tighten then explode away from my now giant, still growing body. Before I lose sight of him in the fabric of the tent ceiling, I lunge for King Thetin and grab him up.

Then my head hits the tent and I thrust it away with one hand, clutching the Trevi king in my other arm. I had hoped we would be outside when I pulled this stunt but I suppose it was naïve to have thought that might happen.

Never mind that now! The cool rain hits my face. I blunder free of the tent and don't waste a second, leaping over the Trevi soldiers who gape at me, ignoring the screams of outrage and fear that come from behind me.

Not towards the town where my comrades huddle in damp besiegement. I race back the way I came, frightening horses and soldiers as I make for the slope where Damir dropped me.

"He has the king! After him!"

Shocked as they are, these Trevi soldiers are no slouches. Arrows whiz by my ankles and hooves thunder as they give chase. Naked, with no armor, I sprint through the mud out of camp.

"I've got him, let's go!" I holler, belting through the trees towards to bald crown of the hill.

A sharp pain in my hand almost makes me drop the Trevi king. Wide-eyed but not panicked, Thetin has worked free a dagger and stabbed me. I'd be impressed if it didn't hurt so much. "Stop that!" I yell, plucking the dagger from him and hurling it away.

My headlong rush up the hill is abruptly arrested as I trip. I have the sense to roll and protect my prisoner rather than squashing him flat.

"Give him here," Damir's bored sounding voice fills me with relief.

"Let me check him for weapons!" I gasp, catching for breath.

Thetin is too stunned by our fall to move for a second. I rip away his sword belt and yank back his lovely dark cloak.

"He's clear!"

Damir's claws encircle the enemy king and the first signs of fear come over his face.

"Keep running!" the dragon urges.

Heaving in air, I roll to my feet and stumble down the hill. Damir lifts off, King Thetin in claw, his face a mask of soundless terror as the ground falls away.

I hear the hooves pounding after me. I run.

~ | ~

Running downhill is significantly more dangerous than running uphill, but that applies to horses as well as men, so my pursuers are just as hampered by the uneven slope, slippery patches and rain-soaked brush. I have scoped the route, however, so while they chase me, I'm not running blind.

Each giant step I take starts to shrink as I scramble west towards the river. This part of the plan is even less certain than stage one or two—the times I'd been awake for the shrinking it happened more slowly than the growing, but I hadn't exactly timed it. I'm also tired, cold and my exertions from escaping the camp leave me wanting to curl up with a bowl of soup under a blanket.

I push on. My feet hit muddy water, suggesting I've hit the edge of the river, though I'm still in the trees. The flooding hadn't looked as bad on this side, but the river clearly no longer resides within its banks.

"There he is!"

Uh oh. I burst free of the trees and wade deeper into the chilly swirl of grey water, scanning the sky for Damir.

He is nowhere to be seen.

"Damir!" I yell. *Shit.* I don't want to retreat to the trees where he can't swoop down and get me, but in the river there is no cover from the spears and arrows coming up fast.

At least naked I don't have any clothes or armor to weigh me down. My balls don't thank me, though, as I flounder deeper and strike for the opposite shore. *This is suicide.*

Something flashes past my head and into the water. An arrow? But the current is already swirling me away from my Trevi pursuers and now my biggest enemy is the river that has just saved me from them.

"Swim!"

My head snaps up. The black dragon crouches on the opposite bank, our prisoner still clutched in his front claws.

"Help!" I try to yell but my limbs are growing heavy. This is far more vicious than the current that swept me from the island. I glimpse Damir taking off, but will he reach me in time?

The rope whacks the surface in front of me then dances away. I sense Damir above, trying to match my pace in the current and I reach desperately for the lifeline. Numb fingers struggle to grasp as I snatch the rope to me and loop it under my arm.

"Go!" I splutter, and pray to the ancestors he's heard, and that I can hold on.

My shoulder wrenches as he lifts me from the river and back towards the bank. I scream and my fingers slip involuntarily. I can't grip any longer. My frozen muscles won't obey.

I fall.

And hit the ground in a tumultuous roll. Twigs snap as I crash through bushes and groan to a halt.

Ughhhhhh.

"Eitel?" Wind from his wingbeats doesn't even chill me, I'm so cold already. "Take off your outer skin, human!" he orders, presumably to King Thetin, since I'm still as naked as the day I was born.

I crack open my eyes to see the terrified Trevi king kneeling in a heap before Damir.

"Take it off!" the dragon barks again.

I groan. "He won't understand you. Hey, your grace, take off your cloak before my dragon friend eats you."

Thetin shoots a frantic look at me and unclips his cloak.

"Toss it here." I heave myself upright. I just want to curl up and sleep but if I don't move I'll die.

He glares, but a growl from Damir prompts him to obey.

I wrap the cloak around me and try to repress my shivers. A draconic hand gathers me up and presses me close. The warmth from his skin seeps into me. I sigh.

"You are bleeding!" Damir snuffles at me. "Where are you hurt?"

"I'm fine!" I wave him away. My hand is a dull throb, numbed by the cold river.

"You seek to assassinate me?" King Thetin demands, a wary eye on Damir. I force myself to watch him carefully, despite my eyelids growing heavy. He might try to run, even though he's on the wrong side of the river from his army.

"No, just take you hostage," I say. Switching to the draconic tongue, I tell Damir. "Let's go. The sooner we get this bastard in front of Prince Gereon and Princess Rhea the better."

I can hear a smile in his voice as he rumbles. "Do not fret, Eitel. I won't let him escape. Are you fit to ride? I can carry you." He sounds anxious.

I give a tired smile back, even though he can't see it. Being carried is very tempting… "It's not far," pride forces me to say. "I can ride."

Eleven

Turns out riding a dragon naked is not something I'd recommend. Fortunately it's a short hop, back over the river but this time to the besieged town.

Caelon is damp, but the clouds hold back their rain in the time it takes to circle, wave for the guards' attention and coast in to land. I know Kamelya and Dorukhan have been delivering supplies but I don't know how comfortable the humans are with giant scaled beasts swooping out of the sky.

No one attacks. Several soldiers actually run up and call out, then halt in confusion.

"Dorukhan?" one queries.

Damir snorts a laugh. "He will be so annoyed you think I'm him." He has a point. Damir isn't as small as say, Axel, but nowhere near as massive as the great black dragon. I don't bother to translate.

"We have King Thetin hostage!" I call, sliding down, trying not to shear my cock off on Damir's scales as I do.

The Medvajan soldiers gape, whether at the furious, red-headed young king in Damir's claws, or my naked ass, I don't know. I hit the ground and stagger, struggling to wrap Thetin's purloined cloak around me and regain some dignity. I'm a much larger man than the king, so the cloak isn't really up to the task.

"Get Prince Gereon!" I flap my free hand, the other clutching the cloak closed. "Get your princess!"

It doesn't take long for the royals to arrive.

"What in all the sweet ancient gods...?" Princess Rhea demands, her long strides eating up the ground as she and her husband, my prince, approach.

"You took Thetin hostage?" Gereon's eyebrows shoot up.

"*King* Thetin," my hostage grinds out. Despite his dishevelment, he holds himself with cold poise.

Princess Rhea is unimpressed. "That would account for all the chaos we've seen in your camp from our walls. The lack of discipline is appalling," she insults.

Thetin bares his teeth, and Damir growls. Everyone falls silent, looking up at the dragon.

"Escort *King* Thetin to a secure chamber," the princess orders. "Make sure he is unharmed, and unable to cause harm, to himself or others." Several of her soldiers snap to attention and bow, then form an escort around the Trevi king, hands on their swords. The red-head sneers, then shoots me an evil look. "I'd ask for my cloak back, but it has been sullied."

I grin slowly. "I shall have it laundered for you, Your Grace." Elation grows as he is escorted away. *I can't believe we pulled this off!*

Prince Gereon clears his throat. "I don't believe we've had the pleasure." He gives a polite bow to Damir.

I glance up in time to see the dragon nod then look at me. "Eitel, what did this human say?"

"Ah, of course." I translate. It's a pity we didn't get Kyan to work the spell of tongues on Damir before we left, but that might have given away our plan and we might have been stopped.

"I am Damir, of Obsidian Clan. You must be the prince to which Eitel is so dutiful. He does you credit."

I omit this last bit, embarrassed, but Gereon takes in my barely cloaked nakedness and nods seriously. "My dear, this is one of the volunteers who went west with Kyan," he says mildly to Princess Rhea, who is still glaring after King Thetin. "I trust the others are well?" he asks me.

"Quite well, Your Highness." I bow deeply, causing some sniggers to erupt from behind me. I grimace.

"How did you manage to snatch him?" Princess Rhea bows elegantly to Damir. "We had hoped for aid but had been given to understand it was to remain non-violent. We haven't seen Kamelya or Dorukhan in almost two days—we presumed they took leave to hunt but nothing was said."

I don't have the skill of an interpreter so I wait until she's finished and give him a summary.

Damir shakes his head. "Your enemy ambushed them somehow, and Dorukhan was injured. Kamelya took him back to the Weyr to be treated. The council was... quite agitated."

I glance around at all the soldiers, conscious that his words could cast the wrong impression.

"Dorukhan and Kamelya were ambushed and injured. They are back at the Weyr." I clear my throat. "I asked Damir to bring me back. I thought if we could capture King Thetin we might be able to negotiate a truce."

Murmurs of surprise.

"Are they displeased?" Damir asks, his voice low.

"I don't think so," I shoot back. "I focused on how you brought me back to capture King Thetin."

Damir nods. "Ah. It is true. Eitel insisted on returning and carrying out this brave plan. I merely assisted. He infiltrated the enemy camp at great risk to himself and took the king hostage."

I hesitate. I don't want to translate that.

"What did he say?" Princess Rhea asks.

I cough. "Damir was instrumental in carrying out this plan. I couldn't have infiltrated the Trevi camp without his help."

I see Phoenix out of the corner of my eye. I hadn't noticed until now that he was one of the soldiers present. He looks impressed, but it's somehow not important to me now. I fix my gaze firmly on Prince Gereon, who sighs.

"Someone get this man a pair of trousers. You, you and you—ensure the sentries are on high alert in case the Trevi try to launch a rescue."

"And a chair, and something to eat," Princess Rhea adds, her assessing gaze taking in my tired face and cold form.

Caelon is a town used to the winter rains, so most of the buildings around the square have large overhangs, and it is to one of these we move.

Damir is curled up behind me, unbothered by the drizzle that has re-established itself. He tries to insist I must see a medic for my stabbed hand, but I shush him, embarrassed, so he refuses to move from my back until my report to the Prince and Princess is done.

They question me quickly and quietly, these royals who seem to work so well as a team. They tease the details out of me. Neither seem surprised at my mention of the enchanted tear and the magic it enacted, though I thought I saw Gereon smirk briefly. *Does the prince dream of dragons too?*

At one point, a Medvajan captain called Lord Cahill joins us. "I've questioned King Thetin," he informs the royals. "He wasn't particularly polite at first, but when I told him that our lookouts could spot infighting happening in their camp, it took all the wind out of him." He hesitates. "Their kingdom is a mess. Crop failures, warlords rampaging all over the place."

The princess nods. I slump back in my chair, grateful for the spare clothes and boots I'm now dressed in. Damir's presence is reassuring and the hot toddy I'm clutching warms my insides. I want to curl up with him and sleep.

"We know about the warlords." Princess Rhea purses her lips. "He united them against us."

"Turns out he originally had plans to offer marriage to you, Rhea," Captain Cahill says. "But they wouldn't have a bar of it, all wanting him to marry their daughters instead. He turned that on them, however, promising marriage to the house of whichever general helped him win lands to the south."

"Ah." Prince Gereon furrowed his eyebrows in consternation. "So they all joined together in an effort to out-compete the others?"

"It's distracted them," Captain Cahill agrees. "He's barely more than a boy, but he's sharp as a tack, and he's sitting on a nest of anthills with those warlords. But he's the only one who can manage to stop them slaughtering each other and his people dying in the process."

"Hmm." Princess Rhea considered. "Why don't we let Eitel get some rest and put our heads together about how to best work this to our advantage. Thetin wants unity. We want peace. While he's our guest, let's convince him that looks the same."

I yawn, then cover it quickly. Gereon smiles. He's still so handsome but somehow I don't have that same longing.

"You are dismissed, Eitel. Get some sleep."

I stand and bow deeply. "Forgive me, Your Highnesses, but at some point I'd like to return to the Weyr. I know the dragons are reluctant to become militarily involved, but the Trevi don't know that, and I'd like to keep building the friendships there." I can't help but reach back and touch Damir on the neck when I say this, and both royals and Captain Cahill exchange a look. *What did I say?*

Princess Rhea looks at me, then Damir, and smiles—a mysterious, unreadable smile. "I support this, if my dear husband does."

Gereon nods, a sparkle in his eyes. "Absolutely. You will need to return and report periodically, as part of your duties, but I see great benefit in having a more permanent envoy. We will discuss this also."

"Thank you, Your Highnesses." I bow again and salute Captain Cahill. I turn to Damir, who regards me with a calm gaze. "I need to sleep. I'll come and find you. They've said I can return to the Weyr but will need to report back from time to time."

"I will bring you as often as you like," he vows. "I would like to see more of your lands." He butts my chest affectionately.

I turn to leave the overhang and see my cousin Jep, standing at ease. I give him a tired smile and salute.

"Sergeant."

"Come on, soldier." He looks at me, then at Damir, and shakes his head. "I'll show you where we're billeted. Then you can tell me what in all the ancestors you managed to get yourself into now."

Damir narrows his eyes. He may not understand Jep's words but his exasperated tone translates itself.

"Does this human have a problem with you, Eitel?" he rumbles warningly.

Jep flinches and takes a step back. I rest my hand on Damir's snout. "It's fine. This is my cousin, Jep. He's my sergeant."

This doesn't help. Damir growls. "The one who says you are stupid?"

"Damir!" I'm too tired to mediate. "It's alright. He's just taking me somewhere to sleep."

Damir huffs through his nose. "You would be safer with me." But he subsides.

"Eitel…" Jep ventures, not taking his eyes off the dragon.

"It's fine, Jep." I yawn. "Damir is just being protective." I smile and pat Damir on the nose. He shakes his head, then leans back into my hand.

"I'll see you soon, I promise," I tell him.

He flicks his eyes to Jep, then me. "Tell your cousin you aren't nearly as stupid as you pretend to be."

"What did he say?" Jep asks as we walk away.

I glance back at Damir, who is curled up in the square, amber eyes still smoldering as he watches us. "He says I'm clearly the better looking and more intelligent one in the family."

Jep's look of incredulity is worth all the aches and tiredness I've acquired. I even believe it a bit myself.

Twelve

It's summer, and the war is over. Princess Rhea and Prince Gereon eventually exchanged King Thetin for a number of Trevi hostages—sons and daughters of all his major lords, to come live in Zivalj at court.

Negotiations took some time, given the state of the roads in winter, but by all accounts Thetin was not displeased with the outcome. His lords are obliged to behave to ensure their children's safety and comfort, and he is obliged to behave so Princess Rhea doesn't send one of those children home and thus enable that lord to raise his banner against his king. A neat solution.

A dragon in the sky above Medvaja or Huon is not an unheard of sight now, though still very exciting for the people below. If you look hard, sometimes there are riders on those dragons, and sometimes I'm one of them.

Turns out I quite like flying when I'm not airsick, and I especially like getting to visit my family back in Huon, but I live in the Weyr most of the time. I'm a special ambassador, along with Monique, Nyree and a few adventurous nobles and merchants from both countries. We've got our own small weyr, large enough to accommodate dragons but modified to be comfortable for humans.

I prefer to live with Callistemon and Damir, and Monique stays with Kamelya when she's there. We all travel back and forth, arranging trades and conveying messages when convenient. It's very much done on the Weyr's terms—no dragon has been enticed to live east of the mountains yet, but Damir quite enjoyed meeting my family and we go back there often. I've been living in Jep's shadow my whole life, so my parents were quite astonished and proud of how I've risen. It embarrasses me when they boast to their neighbors. I try to tell them I didn't volunteer that rainy night to be brave, I just did it without thinking, but Damir doesn't help. Now that Kyan has performed the spell of tongues on him, he loves to reenact the capture of King Thetin and has everyone agog.

My sister has become quite fond of him—she was frightened at first, as was everyone in the village, but he was very careful and gentle, and now she runs out every time we come in to land. She can't hear us, but she seems to have some sort of extra sense about when we are arriving.

She also is the only one who knows Damir and I are more than just friends. Most of the humans we visit are still getting their heads around the fact that dragons are not just giant flying lizards, but hopefully with the work we do that will change one day.

I even get to visit the Medvajan capital, Zivalj, whilst reporting to Princess Rhea and Prince Gereon. Captain al Stauberg has converted a section of palace gardens into a pavilion for visiting dragons so I fall under her jurisdiction during my visits. I don't mind. It's nice to have someone else do the thinking for me from time to time, particularly when I need to be diplomatic and polite when visiting towns and villages across the land.

Lucky I've always been good at making people like me, only this time I'm not keening for their affection. Damir says he doesn't mind if I want to sleep with other men, but even after the scent-marking wears off, I find I don't really want to. Now and then, just for fun, but it's never as good as it is with him.

"Are you ready?" I ask him. We are in a cave in the mountains, a secret lovers' retreat not far from the western foothills of Medvaja. Damir eyes the enchanted tear I hold out and nods.

"I trust you," he says, and swallows the tear.

As the shrinking spell takes effect, he twines himself around me. I stagger at first under his weight but when he reaches my size it is easy to hold him.

Carefully, lovingly, I unwrap his limbs and tail and lay him gently on the pelts we'd stashed here previously. Belly up, wings splayed, he is vulnerable, but his cock emerges eagerly and I stroke myself, excitement building.

"Hold them together," he begs.

I chuckle. He loves me working us both. Loves the feel of my stiffness against his writhing member. It always seems to have a mind of its own—sometimes teasing, sometimes explorative, but mostly desirous of being touched, sucked, squeezed. It demands my attention and I obey, bracing myself over him.

Each stroke builds heat in my palm, our cocks throbbing, pressed together. I can't wait anymore. I move back, still jerking myself as my other hand takes him up and guides his length into my mouth.

Damir growls, back arching. Dragons might lick but my human mouth works wonders when it comes to sucking. It's hard to keep a rhythm on myself and him so I abandon myself to his pleasure.

"Eitel!" he hisses, but I can already taste his seed and I swallow him down. Another novelty for dragons, one that drives him wild.

I smile as I meet his beautiful, cat-like eyes. Still shuddering, he twists onto his belly, wings raised. I trail my nails down the delicate membrane—sending shivers of delight through his sinuous body.

Kneeling behind him, I nudge his tail aside and make ready to claim him. As well as the pelts, blankets and food I've stored in our cave, a jar of olive oil is an expensive but delightfully helpful addition, and one I don't stint on when it comes to these magical moments alone.

"Yesss," Damir hisses again, as I ease my way in, inch by careful inch. He pushes back, making me moan as his warmth grips me.

He trusts me, and it's beautiful. I fuck him, and it's wonderful. I cant my hips with increasing rhythm, gripping the base of his wings while his tail lashes in desperate pleasure. Pressure builds in my balls and the world focusses to a single point.

And then… ecstasy. I cry out as his roar reverberates my very being. Heat and release and utter abandonment—collapsing in a tangle of tail and arms, wings and legs. Wound together, full of each other's scent and seed and desire.

We may not look the same, but we are good together. I have found the thing I craved; excitement and adventure, while also having a sense of home, of belonging.

What more could a man like me ask for?

www.ingramcontent.com/pod-product-compliance
Lightning Source LLC
Chambersburg PA
CBHW021337060726
47591CB00006B/2060

* 9 7 8 1 7 6 4 1 3 7 9 2 8 *